HIJACK
OUR STORY OF SURVIVAL

HIJACK

OUR STORY OF SURVIVAL

LIZZIE ANDERS AND KATIE HAYES

ANDRE DEUTSCH

First published in Great Britain in 1998
By André Deutsch Limited
76 Dean Street
London W1V 5HA
www.vci.co.uk

André Deutsch Limited is a subsidiary of VCI plc

A catalogue record for this book is available
from the British Library.

ISBN 0 233 99301 0

Typeset by Derek Doyle & Associates
Mold, Flintshire.
Printed by WSOY, Finland.

1 3 5 7 9 10 8 6 4 2

To all the innocent victims of
Ethiopian Airways flight ET961

ACKNOWLEDGEMENTS

To our family and friends who have given us love, support and understanding – thank you for everything.

Also to Robert Kirby, for his trust in letting us write this book whilst continuing our travels. It can't have been easy taking our phone calls from the back of beyond.

Thanks to Andrew Croft and a special thanks to Hannah MacDonald and those who have helped to pull this together. Last, but not least, thanks to all the medical staff who took care of us and to whom we will be forever indebted.

CONTENTS

FOREWORD
By Terry Waite

It was a bright clear morning when I recently left Columbia in South America. As the last of the luggage was loaded onto the plane my companion turned to me.

'I always get nervous when I see them taking suitcases back out of the hold,' he said and looked down at the baggage handlers on the tarmac. I smiled, the handlers returned to the main building and we travelled safely. An hour or so later an airliner leaving from the same airport slammed into the mountains five minutes after take off. There were no survivors. Was it a terrorist incident? At the time of writing the cause of the disaster is unknown.

I returned to my home in the countryside and by coincidence found this manuscript waiting for me. It's the story of two survivors of the Air-Ethiopia hijack in November 1996. The plane ran out of fuel and with considerable skill the pilot brought it down in the sea. 127 passengers died. Two years later Lizzie and Katie along with the other survivors and grieving relatives still wait for an adequate explanation of the incident.

Disaster is no respecter of persons. Two high-spirited

young women on the journey of a lifetime are suddenly thrown into the midst of the most frightening circumstances. Although air travel continues to be one of the safest means of transport, terrorism continues to flourish. When the terrorist strikes the innocent suffer.

This book may be read in two ways. It is certainly a fast moving story that is more gripping than many works of fiction. It is also a valuable document with several important messages for different groups of people. Having known very many victims of trauma and to a certain extent experienced something of trauma myself, I continue to be amazed at the ignorance shown by so many towards the problem. Following their ordeal the two young women ran directly into sheer ignorance shown by those who ought to know better. It should be mandatory for Embassy officials and others who have dealings with the public to have a basic knowledge of post-traumatic stress disorder. Alas, as the authors indicate, this hardly seems to be the case.

In disasters, of course, it isn't only the immediate victims who suffer. There is usually an enormous circle of relatives and friends who wait anxiously for accurate information. In their natural desire to get a story quickly, the media all too frequently report partial or inaccurate news which, as the authors show, can cause considerable distress.

To be a victim is to suffer and suffering is always painful. The simple telling of a story is one way by which victims learn to manage a traumatic experience rather than be managed by it. Although there are many unanswered questions concerning the Air-Ethiopia hijack, Lizzie and Katie have told their story and consequently have not only helped themselves but will also help many that need it. It's a compelling read.

Terry Waite, CBE, 1998.

PART ONE
Changing Our Lives

LIZZIE

I t was a muggy evening in June 1987 when Katie arrived at the small Conduit Street office in London's West End for an interview with the managing director of MTV Europe. The company had only just been set up and the station hadn't even appeared on the air.

'I'm here for the interview,' she told me.

The managing director was tied up in a late meeting.

'Would you like a beer?' I asked, knowing that we always had some bottles in the fridge.

A mischievous smile spread over her face, and at that moment we clicked. She drank the beer, did the interview, got the job . . . and the greatest friendship of our lives was born.

I'd been temping at MTV Europe for a couple of months, as general dogsbody and receptionist. Everyone did a number of jobs while the company was establishing itself, just to get the station ready in time for its launch. It was undoubtedly an exciting place to be, and there were only ten of us in those days, which made for a very relaxed atmosphere. We all became close because we all shared the same objective – to create a brand new version of the highly

2

successful MTV, which had become a mighty music business marketing force in the States. The concept was simple: around-the-clock videos, pop news and ideas aimed at young people throughout Europe. At that stage no-one was sure that a European network, broadcast simultaneously across every country, predominantly in English, would appeal to a continent with so many different languages and cultures. Nor could we be certain that youth culture was at the same stage of development as it was in America. But we all believed fervently in what we were doing. The uncertainty of the project – not knowing whether it would be a huge success or an unmitigated disaster – just added to the excitement.

Although the head office was in London, we were to create the impression that MTV Europe didn't come from anywhere in particular. There would be images from all over Europe, as well as from the UK. The belief, or the hope, was that not only did music transcend all language barriers, but that young adults were interested in Europe as an entity. Therefore, MTV would take trends and issues from each country and offer them out across the whole continent. There would be reports on fashion, clubs, movies, news, local artists and environmental issues from Sweden or Spain that would interest the youth of Europe from Holland to Switzerland.

MTV Europe was also keen to take non-political 'world awareness' campaigns very seriously and in between videos there would be information spots reflecting the world's need to address issues like HIV and Aids, racism and environmental issues such as deforestation, the ozone layer, the effects of CFCs, endangered species and pollution. The philosphy was that such moral issues were common ground all over the world and, given MTV's potential influence on the youth of Europe, it was extremely important to cover them.

Music also provided a common ground between countries. Artists such as Madonna and Michael Jackson were already huge stars in Europe and could be featured alongside local performers. Eros Ramazotti in Italy, Bjork in Iceland and Roxette in Sweden all appeared on MTV Europe before they became famous. MTV became a perfect launch pad for local artists wanting to gain exposure outside their own country.

The diversity and avant garde style of programming that MTV Europe intended to provide would mean that the viewer could be offered a broader picture of the music world. Instead of just asking pop stars questions about their latest single, presenters would do something like go shopping with them. A competition was set up where you could win Jon Bon Jovi's house, and Bryan Adams performed in someone's living room. Stars such as Robbie Williams from Take That would become a presenter for a week.

MTV Europe was launched in August 1987. Phone lines were flung open and callers from every country were able to interact live on air with their favourite artists. It was new, different, young, dynamic, fast, interactive, colourful and modern. Perhaps most importantly, there had never been anything like it before, and it quickly became the fastest growing network in the area. Its success was unprecedented.

It was during this time that Katie and I discovered we had a great deal in common. She had grown up in Sunbury-on-Thames, just twenty minutes from where I had lived in Woking. Both are middle-class Home Counties towns – pleasant enough but quiet – so both of us had been keen to escape to London as soon as we left school. Katie lived in Notting Hill Gate, where I had bought a flat. Her father was an architect, mine was a surgeon. She was the middle of three, and so was I.

We began to travel to work together, talking non-stop all the way. We would almost always have lunch together and inevitably go for a drink after work. She met my friends and family and I met hers. Our worlds joined together and we became part of one large, shared social scene, knowing all the same people and going to all the same places.

Katie was 22 and I was 23 and both of us overflowed with enthusiasm. We weren't the least bit fazed by the long hours and hard work we were expected to put in at MTV. We learnt fast and with each new challenge grew more confident that we could handle anything the world – or MTV, at any rate – threw at us.

It was completely removed from the dead-end jobs I'd had when I first arrived in London. The previous year, however, I'd gone travelling in India, taking an overland bus from Streatham to Kathmandu (the lengths people will go to to get out of Streatham . . .). The trip, which took me through Europe, Syria, Jordan, Iran, Pakistan, India and

Nepal, really opened my eyes to a world beyond the southeast of England. The experience had a profound effect on me, and Katie often used to sigh wistfully and say that she would love to see the world too. After leaving school at sixteen, she had worked ever since.

Any cravings for adventure that we might have felt, however, were more than catered for by our employer. Every day brought new experiences, challenges and distractions, and there was hardly time to eat, never mind brood on what else we might have been doing with our lives. Everyone at MTV was in their early twenties and because people were recruited from all over Europe, we were quite a cosmopolitan group. We were also very close, united by our enthusiasm for this new, exciting project. MTV was always fun, even when the pressure was on, mainly because it fulfilled all our expectations and became fantastically successful, winning the respect of the music business world almost immediately. Once the concept had proved itself to be viable, instant growth was inevitable. As the company expanded, those of us who had proved our loyalty and worth at the beginning were able to grow with it.

Katie, who had worked in music publishing and international marketing for Polydor, before joining MTV, already knew something of the world we were being thrown into, but I knew nothing at all. I had to learn quickly but found that I loved this unpredictable, varied world. No two days were ever the same. I liked the fact that anyone could put forward ideas and everyone was happy to pool their resources to achieve the company's goals. The enormous success of the whole concept provided us with extremely happy days. Being in satellite television meant we were at the cutting edge of technology, as well as of the music industry. We were all very proud of what we had achieved.

MTV's launch took place at the Roxy, a notorious club in Amsterdam. We hired a train to take our guests from Victoria to Gatwick, personalising it to reflect the innovative and over-the-top character of the channel. Guests were served champagne by 'cleaners', dressed up and equipped with brooms, dusters and bottles of Pledge. The guests, a little fazed initially, soon got into the spirit of the event – with just a little help from the free alcohol.

At Gatwick everyone was ushered straight through to a departure lounge, where the customs officials were only slightly bemused by the red passport-style invitations, which were stamped with historic musical events such as Woodstock and Live Aid.

Guests included music journalists, television executives and plenty of stars. Katie and I were having a ball. It was extremely hard to believe that we were a part of such a glamorous event, mingling with people we'd only ever seen on *Top of the Pops*. In the Ladies in the airport, we found Boy George re-applying his make-up. He gave my plum-coloured lipstick a sideways glance.

'I like that colour better than this,' he said. 'Can I borrow it?'

After being shown on to two privately chartered planes,

we were flown to Amsterdam. Trying to help out, I served champagne, but made such a mess in the galley that the stewardesses had to ask me to sit down. At the Roxy, we were met by what looked like statues holding trays of Margaritas – the MTV drink – performance artists sprayed silver from head to toe, with strategically placed fig leaves.

The switch which would send the channel out across the airwaves was due to be thrown at midnight and there was a buzz running through the party as the hour drew closer. We could barely contain ourselves – we were finally going to see the product we believed in so much. There was a ten-second countdown and at exactly midnight Elton John walked out on stage and blasted the channel into life with a detonator. The crowd went wild as the screens lit up around the club. A spoof image of the little girl from *Poltergeist* stood in front of a TV set, announcing 'We're here.' Whitney Houston, the first artist to sing on MTV Europe, was almost drowned out by the crowd. She was followed by Dire Straits with 'Money For Nothing', which of course contains the line 'I want my MTV.'

During the evening Katie and I chatted to some of the company's bigwigs who had flown in from the States for the occasion. As we babbled on about how exciting it all was and how much we enjoyed working for MTV, knowing looks began to appear on their faces.

'That feeling won't last for ever,' they warned us. 'Enjoy it while you can. Once the company becomes big time, everything will change.' We weren't in the mood for their gloomy prophesying, and chose to ignore their comments.

We weren't about to let them burst our balloon, and anyway, we knew that things would be different in Europe. It would never be as aggressive or business-orientated as the States, and we were certain that the fun would go on and on for as long as we wanted it to.

I like to think that Katie and I would have had fun wherever we'd worked, though. She could always make people laugh and was confident enough to be able to make fun of herself and her own mistakes. ('I've just cut Robert Maxwell off!' she giggled one day when the notorious tycoon – one of MTV's major shareholders – had called to speak to her boss.) But she is also sweet and charming, full of good advice in a crisis and very generous with her time if anyone needs consoling. She has such a strong character and sharp wit, but she can be extremely sensitive too, which often clashes with her outspokenness. At MTV she often spoke her mind with considerable boldness but afterwards was often concerned that she had overstepped the mark. She could always see the funny side, though, and never seemed to regret anything for long.

Katie would never take anything too seriously. At one particularly dreary rock festival where we were working long, exhausting hours, our spirits were beginning to wane, despite access to the hospitality supplies backstage. Def Leppard were performing on stage when Katie suggested we brighten up the day. Unaware of her intentions but keen for some distraction, I followed her as she armed herself with a camcorder and marched off to Def Leppard's dressing-room door.

'Right,' she told me, giggling. 'You stand over there and act like a presenter.'

I soon twigged on to what she wanted. 'Here we are,' I told my audience, 'standing outside Def Leppard's changing room, and in a minute we'll be going in to experience first-hand that much talked about "heavy metal smell".' Throwing ourselves into our parts, we managed to pass the whole afternoon in this way. That evening we replayed our efforts, giggling hysterically. We replaced the camera before it was missed but didn't remember to wipe the tapes.

We'd forgotten about the whole incident when a producer stopped Katie in the corridor a week later and handed her a tape.

'You were both great and I'm including the material in the programme,' he told her.

Katie rushed off to find me. 'We've been rumbled! Those stupid tapes we made are about to be broadcast all over Europe!' She was half laughing and half hysterical. 'You're gonna be a big star!' She chucked me the tapes and collapsed on the floor, breathless with laughter.

'It's not funny,' I kept saying, over and over again, which only made her laugh more. I couldn't quite get my head round the idea of a programme where the group talked seriously about their musical careers and we cut in with our inane comments.

The producer eventually stuck his head round the door, having watched our terrified performance. 'That'll teach you!' he laughed.

Another occasion found us in Rome because MTV had

run a competition enabling the winner to film Bono and U2 on stage in front of a packed stadium. The winners were from Czechoslovakia and Katie and I spent the afternoon in a hotel, waiting for them to arrive. They were due at three o'clock but hadn't turned up at five.

'What can have gone wrong?' Katie wondered aloud. 'The instructions were simple and I spent hours explaining everything to them.'

When the phone rang, a look of relief came over her face, and then drained away again as she listened.

'Stay exactly where you are,' she shouted into the phone. 'I'll be right down.'

'What's happened?' I asked as she hung up.

'Come on.' Typically, she started giggling. 'We've got to go to the airport. I'll tell you on the way.'

It transpired that the two winners were massive U2 fans and had arrived dressed up as Bono and The Edge. Perhaps unsurprisingly, the Italian immigration officials had been rather suspicious of these strange characters, fresh in from the Eastern bloc.

'We are going on stage with U2,' they had tried to explain.

Clearly not believing this story the Italian officials were preparing to put them straight back on the plane. They had even forbidden them to make any phone calls. One of them, however, (I'm not sure if it was Bono or The Edge) had managed to escape just long enough to put in a call to us.

'Come quickly,' the heavily accented voice had whis-

11

pered down the line to Katie. 'I'm hiding behind plants in a flower shop and have managed to escape.'

By the time we got there, the escapee had been recaptured from behind the foliage and we had to do some fast talking to convince the authorities that they were genuine. As we left, one of the officials shouted after us. 'Any chance of some tickets?'

'Only if you come dressed as Madonna!' Katie shouted back as we jumped into a taxi and headed for the stadium.

There are so many memories and stories from those first years at MTV. Yet whatever we did, I was always the more rational, sensible one, while Katie lived for the moment. The chemistry between us worked because she seemed to lift me while I grounded her. We both appreciated what the other gave to the relationship. That's not to say, however, that Katie didn't think deeply about things. She was clear about who she was and what she believed in. She is fiercely loyal to those she cares about and has always been good at maintaining strong relationships with people.

She was also highly competent at her job. Her outgoing personality enabled her to make friends easily and she began to move up the corporate ladder almost as soon as she joined. The better the company did, the greater the job opportunities that opened up around us. Katie moved into promotions and then marketing, eventually heading her own team of people across Europe as head of consumer/trade marketing. Even then, she was still loved by everyone who knew her. I never heard anyone ever say a bad word about her, ever.

There were, however, a number of things that terrified her. She hated spiders, for instance, and public speaking. She couldn't touch spiders, and if she dreamt about them she would wake up in a panic. To avoid public speaking in the course of her work, she would put her presentations on tape, adding some entertainment and creativity to what could be long and dreary meetings.

She was also scared of flying. As she was promoted she flew more frequently, and was painfully conscious that the more hours she spent in the air, the greater the chance of something happening. She kept hearing stories from friends who had suffered various glitches on aeroplanes, but still nothing actually ever happened to *her*.

'One of my worst fears,' she said to me once, 'is to be in an air crash and to land in shark-infested waters.'

'Well,' I responded glibly, 'I don't think you need to worry about that. The odds against it must be a billion to one.'

She grinned amiably at her own irrationality.

'My greatest fear,' I told her, 'would be coming out of the Ladies at a big music business event, having accidentally tucked my skirt into the back of my knickers, and then walking back to my table with my head held high, thinking everyone was admiring my outfit.'

'Don't worry,' Katie laughed. 'I'd always tell you.'

I never stopped to think how I'd help her out of the shark-infested waters.

The growth of MTV provided career opportunities for me as well. I enjoyed being receptionist and jack of all trades but I was always on the lookout for something I could concentrate fully on – and I was in the perfect place to be considered for jobs that I would never have been qualified to do otherwise. I was given the job of head of 'talent artist relations' and I didn't have a single contact in the business. I didn't even know the telephone numbers of the record companies and had to start by dialling directory enquiries. Once I got through to the switchboards, I asked if I could speak to 'someone who deals with videos and things'. Hardly the most professional of approaches.

It didn't take long, however, to make some contacts and begin to carve a niche for myself. Everything, after all, was new. There had never been anything like MTV before, so to an extent we were making up the rules as we went along.

My job was to convince the record companies that their stars should be appearing on MTV and supplying us with material. It seems amazing now, when no-one would dream of launching a potential hit without making a video to promote it, that only ten years ago the companies actually had to be persuaded that it was a good idea. I didn't find selling too difficult because I believed so strongly in what we were doing, so I soon had contacts everywhere and felt that I knew what I was doing. My confidence grew in leaps and bounds, the job providing me with an opportunity to meet new people and overcome the reserve I'd had since childhood. I had to learn how to 'do the room' at music business functions – something I would never have imagined myself doing. Obviously, it was difficult to begin with, but as my relationships within the industry strengthened it became easier until eventually it was routine.

I'd suddenly found myself at the very centre of the music business, surrounded by pop stars, glamour and a five-star expense-account lifestyle. It was exhilarating. Katie and I worked closely together, usually attending the same events and sharing the experience like two children let loose in a candy store.

Within a few years it was obvious that the concept of MTV was going to work as effectively in Europe as it had in America, and the big stars began to take serious notice of us. We were dealing, on a daily basis, with people like Madonna, Michael Jackson, U2, Sting and Bryan Adams, all of them keen to be part of what was happening. Katie was flying around Europe in private jets with the likes of Phil Collins and Depeche Mode and I was having dinner and establishing working relationships with the likes of Bon Jovi and George Michael.

The perks were amazing: meeting stars, seeing concerts, getting backstage passes, going to after-show parties, being invited to see artists such as Prince or REM perform in small clubs to hand-picked audiences. We saw wonderful things, travelled extensively round Europe and were even flown to New York and Los Angeles on business.

I suppose it was inevitable, however, that the novelty would begin to wear off. Four years down the line, we seemed to be spending most of our time with business acquaintances rather than with friends. We travelled to so many places but often only saw an airport, a meeting room, a venue and a hotel room. It also became apparent that some of our 'friends' were only there because of the help we might be able to give to their new, struggling artists. The many late nights, weekends and bank holidays spent working all began to merge into one and slowly a disillusioning sense of monotony began to set in. There were hundreds and hundreds of new bands waiting to be discovered and in order to do our jobs properly it was important to pay them as much attention as the big stars. We could see three bands a night, seven days a week, and still it wouldn't be enough – and that was just the UK, never mind the rest of Europe. It felt as if MTV was running off with our lives. Because of the success of the company, the amount of staff dramatically increased. Like many expanding businesses, the corridors were full of new faces and the family atmosphere we had in the early days was gone.

We were no longer a group of young people working all hours to launch a TV station that no-one had heard of – we were part of a big, successful company. The warnings that the American executives had given us at the launch rang in our ears. MTV was becoming like any other large corporation and the small company vibes were being crushed under the weight of bureaucracy and big money. Where once it had been fun to work every waking hour, I was stressed and exhausted by the constant demands of a channel which consumed material at a ferocious pace. The learning curve I had been surfing happily along flattened out and I found that a large part of the job had become routine.

Katie was feeling the same and we started moaning to one another, something we would never have predicted. MTV had become part of the grown-up world.

In 1993, London Records, a subsidiary of Polygram, approached me and asked if I would be interested in becoming head of international marketing. I knew nothing about international marketing and the thought of starting at the bottom and mastering a whole new set of skills was very tempting. I was flattered, and felt that if they were prepared to take a risk on me I should be prepared to do the same. After six and a half years, I knew MTV like the back of my hand. It was time for a change.

Moving jobs had barely any effect on my relationship with Katie, despite her being in Camden and me in Hammersmith. We talked to each other at least three times a day and needed virtually no excuse at all to pick up the phone and call.

'I had a dream last night about my teeth falling out,' I'd say.

'Oh, that means something really important,' she'd reply, 'but I can't remember what it is.'

Trivial conversations like that could go on for hours, never covering anything of consequence – it was that type of friendship. If anything of significance *did* happen, though, Katie's number would be the first one I'd dial.

We tried to engineer working together whenever possible. MTV was a useful marketing tool for London Records, and since Katie was now responsible for a large part of the marketing on and off the channel, we had plenty of excuses to devise outlandish concepts which we could pull off together.

When, for instance, I needed to promote East 17's new album, *Steam*, we came up with the idea of a competition where the winner and a friend would be flown to Turkey for a steam bath with the band. Both Katie and I wanted to go to Istanbul – we had both been just about everywhere else in Europe. Here was our chance, so we accompanied them for three days.

Each year Katie had to deal with a big German rock festival. 'Why don't you come too?' she suggested on the phone one morning. 'You've got a band playing there, haven't you? We could organise a competition.'

We threw ideas back and forth for a while and eventually agreed that the winner and a friend could dress up as Elvis Presley and walk out on stage in front of 80,000 people with Faith No More, to promote their album *King For a Day, Fool For a Lifetime*. I don't know how effective it was as a marketing campaign but it allowed us to spend a couple of days away together.

Then Katie met Charlie and it wasn't long before they were inseparable. It wasn't as if we hadn't had boyfriends before, but Katie and Charlie was something different and fitted seamlessly into our circle. He was six foot two and utterly charming – and he seemed to adore Katie. I was delighted to see her so happy and so secure in the relationship. Charlie was an art dealer, and his knowledge of contemporary art opened up new worlds to us. He would take us round London's galleries, a couple of naïve pupils struggling to understand what modern art was all about. We were defeated when we were confronted with a piece of string hanging off a wall, but on many occasions we were inspired.

Katie's world naturally began to move in a different direction because she visited galleries and openings on a regular basis. But it wasn't just that she had taken up a new interest. She was starting to think more deeply about her life and what she was doing with it. She thought she should find a new direction – something that would lead to greater fulfilment.

'I feel like some perennial plant,' she told me one day as we discussed what it meant to us to be approaching the dreaded 30. 'Every year I do the same thing – all the same planning and the same music events. It's getting boring. I want to be like some enormous oak tree, with strong roots and branches which spread into every space, chasing the light. Charlie's shown me things outside the music business and the more I learn the more I want to learn.'

When I actually had the time to stop and think about it, I had to agree with her. Our lives had become completely dominated by the music industry and our diaries were so crammed with business engagements that we had forgotten there was anything else going on in the world outside. Whenever we sat down to talk, we always returned to the same subject. It was as if we were going over the same ground in an attempt to clarify it in our minds – to bring ourselves to a point where we had worked out how we wanted to change things and move forward. There had to be more to life than what we had discovered so far, but we were still unable to see how to find it. We were also afraid of losing what we had. The months went past and, like most people, we had changed nothing in our lives.

In July 1995, the phone rang on my desk, as it did a hundred times a day. I snatched it up, thinking a dozen different things at once, and heard my father's voice.

'Sit down, Lizzie,' he said. I did. 'I'm afraid your sister is dead.'

Somewhere in my mind I knew it must be true, but I couldn't believe this was actually happening. I felt numb; unable to feel anything. All the activity in the office around me faded into the distance. 'I'll be home as soon as possible,' I said.

Carolyn was 33 years old when she committed suicide. She hadn't been well for a long time, having suffered from depression which had led to several nervous breakdowns. She had threatened to kill herself before but I had never imagined she would actually do it. Nothing like this had ever happened to me before and I wasn't sure how to cope with it. I automatically phoned Katie. She was the only person I wanted to speak to; the only one I could possibly share the pain with. Through my tears I told her the news. My throat felt like it wanted to close up in order to stop the words coming out. Katie cried too.

When I felt strong enough, I stood up and walked away from my desk, leaving it covered with all the things which had seemed so desperately important just a few minutes before. I made my way home, feeling like I had been asleep for a long time and had just woken to face the truth. My thoughts were confused, my emotions a blur. It was as if I had been on a supersonic train, hurtling along at an unbelievable speed. Everything inside the train was clean, chromed and air conditioned: all mod cons but man-made and artificial. Suddenly, I had been pushed off the train. I was sitting in a field of grass and wild flowers. The train had vanished, just leaving the tracks. For the first time in ages I could feel what was real: the warmth of the sun on my skin, the smell of flowers, the sound of the breeze. I was in shock and grieving, but in trying to evaluate death I suddenly felt alive.

I was struck with the thought that Carolyn, although ill, had shown more courage and strength than anyone I had ever met. She had done what she wanted to do with absolute conviction. I could never have done that. I was angry because her actions had plunged my family into despair, but I could only respect her for following the path she had so wanted to go down.

The weeks that followed, with all their rituals and tears, forced me to think more deeply than ever before about everything I could do to make more of my life. There had to be something better than the misery Carolyn had borne. I was determined to live my life to the full; to experience as much as possible; to take whatever risks were necessary in order to do the things I wanted to do. I didn't want to go on doing just one thing with my life. Although I admired the conviction with which Carolyn had acted, the negativity of it seemed all wrong. I wanted my life to be positive.

Over the following gruelling months, Katie was the best friend I could have hoped for. She talked me through it all, suffering with me. Things were never quite the same again; everything was now more grown up and less innocent. Our conversations grew more and more intense and serious. Over and over again we talked about our philosophies of life and what we wanted from it. The facades of glamour and money which surrounded our working lives now seemed to be masking a shallow, tawdry and unhappy reality. Too many people, particularly in the music industry, create illusions as to who they are, becoming selves or egos which are light years away from the real person. We both agreed that we couldn't end up like that – if it wasn't already too late.

We spent endless hours over bottles of wine and mugs of coffee trying to work out what it was in life that made us happy. Was it the brand new BMWs that came with our jobs? The mobile phones? The lap-tops? The business-class air tickets and the five-star hotels? The champagne and the bottomless expense accounts? None of these things were actually *ours*. They were all paid for by our companies and would disappear the next day if we resigned.

None of these frills or perks were real. Never in a million years could we have afforded to stay at the George V in Paris, the Water Tower in Cologne or the Royalton in New York if we had had to foot our own bills. And as much as we enjoyed our glamorous lifestyles, we needed to discover more than where the next bottle of champagne was coming from.

We wanted to give something back to society. Humanitarianism seemed far more important than the profit and loss accounts of the businesses we were part of. And it wasn't even as though companies like ours existed because there was a real passion for music. We realised that the bigger a business got, the less compassion there was for the human spirit and the more hard-nosed people became towards squeezing the last drop of profit out of every opportunity.

At around that time, I went on a trip to Canada with East 17, during which I had to try to persuade them to cram a few more interviews into their already overcrowded schedules. Tony Mortimer, one of the band members, turned to me and asked, 'Why do you do what you do?'

I was silenced, unable to come up with an honest answer which would satisfy either him or me. He was right to question what I was doing; not to take it for granted that I should be pushing and hassling them to get another ounce of publicity. I was now 30 and there had to be more to my life than trying to force musicians to sell another few records. It suddenly seemed so trivial and pointless.

It wasn't long after this that Katie took a positive step towards making the change we both needed. She told me she couldn't continue doing her job for much longer. She felt overly cushioned and protected by the environment we worked in. Her conscience was beginning to prick. She had been at MTV for ten years and nothing about it was new to her any more. It would have been easy to stay there, however – there was little doubt she would become more and more successful at what she did. But was that what she really wanted?

'I want to be able to put my head on my pillow at night with a clear conscience, knowing that I've done something worthwhile,' she said. 'There are all these people working for organisations like Greenpeace, The Red Cross and Save the Children; and all we have to worry about at work is who's at number one and what Pamela Anderson's up to.'

I knew I felt the same way. Perhaps it was my age, but the idea of attending a rock concert was becoming less appealing than the idea of spending a quiet weekend in the country with real friends. Deep down, though, I knew it wasn't because I was getting old. The truth was, I was frightened of what I'd become. Working in the music business had changed me. It was a tough world and I had hardened up to deal with it. I had to be aggressive in order to get things done, and that had been effective, but now I began to question the ethics of what I was doing. It was like a spiritual awakening. I discovered, when I studied myself closely, that I had become someone who wasn't really me. It had been a slow metamorphosis, but I had turned into a busy corporate executive. The process had been so gradual that I hadn't noticed it happening; so seductive that I had actually enjoyed much of it. A voice inside my head was warning me that I should stop and think about what was happening before it was too late to go back.

The more deeply I thought about my own future, the more the image of the fast, shiny train with all its mod cons stuck in my mind. I was still trapped in those rich, clean carriages and if I wasn't careful I would still be hurtling forward in ten years' time. And I would have missed every bit of the world which had passed by outside the windows while I was so busy inside.

I talked to Katie about my fears. What if I didn't like the station which the train finally pulled into? It would be too late to go back and retrace my steps. The balance in my life was all wrong and I didn't like the aggressive, cynical person I was becoming. I seemed to be giving all the time and not getting anything back. I had to constantly inspire others in order to push forward new projects, and I felt drained by the effort of it all and disappointed by the super- ficiality of my daily goals. Listening to music on the radio was no longer a pleasure. It was my work, and I suddenly resented that.

On the other hand, my employers had never given me anything to complain about. They gave me all the opportu- nities I could ask for, and backed me financially and practi- cally in everything I wanted to do. I knew that it was a wonderful job, something that millions of other people would consider themselves lucky to have, and I began to wonder if I was just being ungrateful and greedy. Did I deserve to get any more from life? Wasn't I already getting more than the vast majority of people? But if I wanted to continue my career I had to be sure that I could commit myself to it 100 per cent, and I was no longer sure that I could do that.

In April 1996, Katie was given a week's free skiing trip to Tignes in France as a Christmas bonus. She always enjoyed being in the mountains – for Katie they provided a perspective on life. They gave a view of the world which showed the clearest path. Standing above the world, it seemed easy to avoid the complexities of daily life in the valleys below.

She too wanted to stand tall and not be confused by the intricacies of fast, modern living. She wanted to become calm, with a clear, simple view of her goals. The air in the mountains was always clean and unpolluted and left her feeling strengthened by the peace and quiet. She believed that the force which had created them also energised her.

One evening while on this holiday, Katie found herself chatting to a young Israeli guy who was just out of the army. They clicked immediately and conversation was easy. Inevitably, they fell into a discussion about life and what they wanted from it. Coming from the war-torn Middle East, his stories made the music business seem even more insignificant. For Katie, his clear vision and philosophies on life were a revelation, and she discussed the possibilities of travelling the world, explaining the insecurities she felt about leaving her work and the comfort zone of London. She was impressed by his strength of character and his willingness to go after things that were important to him without worrying about the future. He made everything seem possible.

It was over the following days, skiing over the crisp white snow under the stunning blue skies, that Katie decided she was going to change her life. She began to formulate a plan, looking for a way in which she could be proactive rather than remaining on the treadmill. She was going to give up everything and travel the world, certain that once she was able to see what was happening around her, and once she got to know herself better, it would become obvious which path she should follow. She asked Charlie if he would travel with her.

Charlie, however, did not feel the same way. He wasn't battling with his conscience or having doubts about his career. He was doing something he loved and didn't want to change his life. Giving up what he had wouldn't have made him happy. He declined Katie's offer but completely supported her decision.

Now that she had decided on a way forward, Katie wasn't going to be deterred by anything. If Charlie couldn't go with her she would find someone else, and I was the obvious next target. We met for a drink and soon got on to that same subject which preoccupied both of us more than any other. To begin with, I thought we were still talking hypothetically, as we had been for months, but it gradually dawned on me that Katie was now serious. She had worked out a feasible scenario for effecting all the changes we both needed. I began to think about the logistics of what she was suggesting. The more I thought about it, the more it made sense.

We arranged to meet for another of our normal after-work drinks, both knowing that from now on things were going to be different. No more complaining about our lives and our lack of direction. No more daydreaming and fanta-sising. We had suddenly become bored with hearing ourselves – all negative talk and no trousers! Now we had to actually decide what we were going to do next. We had to plan our way forward, step by practical step.

Taking a year off work to travel the world would give us the time we needed to think, question our lives and consider our options. Did we want to have children? Did we want to marry? Did we want careers? What did we really believe was important? What purpose did we actually want to have?

There was never going to be a better time. We had no responsibilities, except for ourselves, and we had enough money, if we sold everything and pooled our resources, to support ourselves for twelve months. We did not have any expectations – we just wanted to lay ourselves open to any opportunities that might offer themselves to us.

The best things in life happen when you're not expecting them, we reasoned, and no expectations means no disappointments. If we took a few risks we would feel more aware of our lives, more awake to everything going on around us. Life should be like a game of chess – always keeping you on your toes.

Why had it all seemed so confusing before. It was so simple and obvious now that we had made the decision. What had we got to lose? What was a year, anyway? We were excited, resolute and happy. We had regained the spontaneity of our early days at MTV. We had retaken control of our lives.

Of course, we still had our moments of worry: 'What will we do when we get back?' 'The money won't last for ever.' 'Will we look back in a year's time and realise it was all a huge mistake?' 'What career opportunities are we likely to miss by doing this?'

But because there were two of us, we were always able to talk each other out of these momentary panics. Ultimately, we had to decide to follow our hearts and not our heads. It felt like the right thing to do, even though we couldn't justify it rationally, and that had to be enough. Whatever happened, we were going to be learning something new every day – even if that lesson was that we were making a huge mistake. We were going to find out about other ways of life, other environments – things and places we had never had time to think about – and we were going to enjoy and savour every moment.

Through experience we had learnt about the music business and now we wanted to do the same with the rest of our lives. When I thought back to how exhilarating it had been to travel to India ten years before, I was suddenly impatient for more of the same. We both craved adventure, risk and perhaps even a little danger.

Overnight we had acquired a new goal in life. We felt nervous about telling our friends – would they think we were mad? – but when we plucked up the courage we received only positive feedback. It was clear that deep down lots of people nursed similar dreams of escape and freedom. Disillusionment seemed to be a part of so many of our friends' lives, but they were happy for us to walk the plank first before taking the plunge themselves. The huge amount of support we were given increased our convictions that we were doing the right thing. Nobody tried to talk us out of it or even question our motives. Perhaps it made sense to them, too: if you're not happy, change things. It's as simple as that – or it should be. It's easy to have dreams and ideals when you're young, but social pressures make it harder as the years pass. It takes a great deal of courage to keep pursuing your dreams as you grow older. By the time you have reached 30, it's not always seen as responsible to give up a good job and set off around the world. Society expects you to settle down and bring up children. But if we had never learnt to take care of ourselves, how could we take care of anybody else? Surely, in the bigger scheme of things, that was the more responsible thing to do – and perhaps the people we talked to saw the truth in that.

For the next few months, we spent our weekends looking at rucksacks, mosquito nets, sleeping bags, insect repellents, hiking boots, thermals, sunglasses, sweatshirts and fleeces. We investigated prices at Trailfinders. We went to the doctor to get the right jabs.

The shopping, as shopping usually is, was fun, but the more we thought about swapping the luxury of our expense-account lives for the rigours of back-packing, the more we wondered whether it might not be too great a culture shock to handle in one go.

'Why don't we ease ourselves into it a bit?' I suggested. 'We could take an overland trip first.' My reason was that it would be like a halfway house. We would be driven around in a truck so we wouldn't have to deal with the rigours of travelling under our own steam, and we'd be with a group of people rather than completely on our own. They would supply tents, food, itineraries and all the other things we'd need. We would be camping and still have to pull our weight, but we wouldn't have to deal with all the responsibilities of travelling independently.

Katie agreed, so we went to an open evening for Encounter Overland in Earls Court Road, who claimed that their trips were 'adventures not holidays'. We liked what we heard so it was just left to us to decide which of their trips to go on. After lengthy discussions, we decided on spending three months going overland from Kenya to Cape Town. We put our names down on the waiting list.

Once we had arrived in Cape Town, we would feel ready to carry on alone. We would then go on to India, Thailand, Vietnam, Laos, Cambodia, Malaysia, Indonesia, Australia and New Zealand. To finish the trip off, we would buy a purple VW camper van in Los Angeles and drive it across the USA to New York – a dream come true.

We wanted to visit every continent. We wanted to learn about things from a different perspective: new cultures, places, people, religions, foods, ways of living, landscapes, smells, sounds, ways of dressing, modes of transport, languages, histories, sunsets and sunrises. We wanted to see full moons and clear, starry skies and talk with people whose lives had been completely different to ours. We wanted to see the Taj Mahal, the Himalayas, the Wats of Laos, the beaches of Thailand, the jungles of Malaysia, the Angkor Wat of Cambodia, the new post-war Vietnam, the tribes of Africa, the deserts of Australia, the untouched beauty of New Zealand, the orangutans of Sumatra and the Komodo dragons.

We also wanted to experience the sheer vastness and diversity of America. Having only visited Los Angeles, New York and Miami, there was a great deal in between which we wanted to see. It would make sense to buy our own van – not something shiny and new, but something old, basic and reliable, with a few miles on the clock (a bit like us, really). We wanted purple because we could. In our minds we had no restrictions – and purple seemed to symbolise the fact that we could have anything in our newfound freedom. Wherever we parked would be our home and we could go wherever we wanted.

'Nairobi to Cape Town is a very popular route,' the woman at Encounter Overland warned us. 'You need to book straight away if you want to get on it.'

We couldn't act quickly because we still had to sort things out. One of our biggest concerns was selling Katie's flat. By the time that had gone through, the trip was fully booked. Encounter Overland suggested an alternative that went from Nairobi up through Northern Kenya into Ethiopia. It was a brand new itinerary for them and they were the only company that ran it. The trip was only a month long but when we went away to think about it, we both agreed that one month might be a better length of time to spend with a group of people we hadn't even met yet. Within a few days, Encounter Overland had debited the whole amount for the trip from our accounts. There was no going back now!

We booked the air tickets, arranged our visas and bought travel insurance for a year. Charlie would look after my flat. The only thing left to do was pluck up the courage to tell our bosses that we were leaving. Katie took the plunge first. Completely shocked, MTV initially tried to talk her out of it. They offered her both a sabbatical and a promotion in an attempt to induce her to stay, but her mind was made up. Eventually, they had to accept her resignation as final. There was nothing wrong with her job, so there was nothing they could do to make it better.

I was desperate to leave London Records on good terms, not knowing whether in a year's time I might be back and looking for work. I kept putting the moment of truth off until our travel deadlines made it impossible to delay any longer. I made an appointment with the managing director and awkwardly blurted out, 'I want to leave.'

He was obviously startled. I explained about our travel plans. 'What are you running away from?' he asked, when I had finished.

'I think,' I replied, 'that if I stayed I would be running away from what I really want to do. It's sometimes easier not to do things you want in life.' He realised that I was not to be dissuaded.

Next, we set about the serious business of buying identical pairs of all the things we had identified as necessary to our survival. We laughed at the idea of having these 'uniforms'. 'If we end up in some remote area of the world, people will see two English girls wearing identical outfits and think there's an army of us just around the corner,'

Katie joked. The idea appealed to us and we kept on shopping.

Someone once told me that rituals are important in civilisation because they mark the point where something has finished and something new is starting. So we had leaving parties to attend, at which there were numerous speeches telling us how much we would be missed. Katie was given Hilton Hotel vouchers by MTV to spend around the world – for those days when we wanted to indulge ourselves a little and escape from the harsh realities of the travelling life – and we both knew we wouldn't say no to a bit of luxury now and then. I was given money.

The last thing Katie worked on for MTV was a George Michael Unplugged. She was a huge fan, and knowing that I would enjoy it too, she invited me along. It was a fantastic way to spend our last night before we stepped out into the unknown.

There were other colleagues from MTV there and we chatted about our plans. 'We're going to write a book together, all about our experiences,' we told one person. 'We're going to call it *The Trip* and write alternate chapters.' He laughed but we just smiled back. 'You'll see!'

Saying goodbye to our families was difficult, particularly as some of them seemed rather confused by what we were doing.

'You're going travelling the world?' Katie's grandmother in Bristol said. 'So we'll be seeing you on the news, then?' She had lived in the same place for most of her life and it was as though she thought we were the first people to do a round-the-world trip. But how horribly prophetic her innocent words were to prove.

We had compiled a post restante itinerary of places we would be stopping off at and handed it out to anyone who said they wanted to keep in touch. Katie, having sold her flat, had moved into mine with Charlie and we had spent the last two weeks in a whirl of last-minute arrangements and irritating details. We had packed, and then packed again. My sister Carolyn had written a letter to each member of the family before she died and I still hadn't quite found the right moment to open mine. I had been holding on to it, unopened, for a year. I decided to pack it and when we reached somewhere wonderful on the trip and I had the time to read it and think about her clearly, I would open it.

It was evening and there was a full moon in the sky as we said our final goodbyes and headed for the BA flight to Nairobi. Setting off on our adventure was like turning the page of a particularly exciting book. The last ten years was a chapter which was now over, and we had no idea what would happen in the next. It was a heady mixture of freedom and anticipation.

We had promised to keep in weekly contact with our families, assuming that we would be able to find working phones wherever we were – this was 1996, after all. Katie and Charlie said a tearful goodbye. He had been very supportive of the trip and understood her need to travel, but that didn't make parting any easier. He was already planning to meet us in five weeks in India, the first of many staggered visits we were to receive from him as we moved around the globe.

We couldn't help but grin at each other when we stepped off the plane in Nairobi. We had dreamed of this moment so many times and now we had a whole year of arriving in new places ahead of us. We had talked endlessly about our trip for the past few months, but we could never have been wholly prepared for how exhilarating it actually felt.

The airport was awash with chaos and we felt conspicuously clean and new with our immaculate rucksacks and freshly bought outfits. We were tired from the overnight flight but emerged happily into the early morning sunshine outside. There were people everywhere and all of them seemed to be shouting at us.

'Want a taxi? Want a taxi?' A hundred voices clamoured for our attention at once. We had been warned that bandits sometimes attacked the roads outside Nairobi and our beginners' caution drew us towards the huge smile of the woman overseeing the government taxi service.

The early morning air was warm and hazy as we were driven into town, and the Miramar Hotel – where the Encounter Overland trip was starting from – was actually quite nice, which was a pleasant surprise. We strode boldly into the reception, both keen to get to our room and catch up on our sleep.

'We're due to join the Encounter Overland trip,' I announced to the woman behind the counter.

'I'm afraid Encounter haven't booked any rooms,' she

replied, pointing to a notice posted on the other side of the lobby. 'Encounter Overland party to meet in the bar at 5.00 pm – Yo-Yo, your driver,' we read.

'We can't sit around all day, just waiting,' I said, feeling suddenly exhausted. 'I need sleep.'

'Let's take a room for the day, then,' Katie suggested. So much for being careful with our money! 'That will give us a chance to sort our stuff out and leave what we don't need here, ready for when we go on to India.'

I certainly wasn't going to argue. And anyway, we had to wean ourselves off our old lifestyles gently, I decided . . .

We repacked half our stuff into one of the rucksacks and asked the genial receptionist to put it in the lock-up for us, along with all our onward tickets and most of our money. This way, if we were attacked in Africa, we wouldn't lose everything and would still be able to continue on the next leg of our journey. As we locked the door on our possessions, we told her we would be back in a month to pick everything up.

'We'll see you then,' we said cheerily.

'I hope so.' She smiled sincerely, no doubt alluding to the possibility of us meeting with bandits. We didn't allow the thought to worry us, and headed to our beds for the day – a luxury we wouldn't have again for some time.

At five o'clock we stationed ourselves in the bar and watched keenly as our seven fellow travellers began to appear around us. We were all a little apprehensive, so it was left to Yo-Yo, our 25-year-old driver, to break the ice.

'I'm half Israeli and half French,' he told us.

'Why is there no booking at the hotel for us?' I asked, as soon as the introductions were out of the way. 'Where do we stay tonight?'

'We don't need a hotel,' he said cheerfully. 'We're camping.'

'Camping?' Naturally, we were just a bit startled. 'In the city?'

'Yes, of course.' Yo-Yo seemed oblivious to our concern.

'Is that safe? Isn't it true that the place is known by the locals as Nairobbery?' Katie enquired.

Yo-Yo laughed his most charming laugh, 'Oh, don't worry! You'll be OK.'

After a brief chat about the rules of the trip and the route we were planning to take, Yo-Yo led us out to the blue and orange Encounter Overland Bedford truck parked outside the hotel.

We piled in, already bored of lugging a heavy rucksack around, and as we headed for the camp site, the rain began to fall. Both Katie and I felt our spirits sinking for the first time. I'm not sure what we'd imagined but it certainly wasn't this.

At least our tent had already been erected when we arrived at the site. A vegetable stir fry was sizzling uninvitingly beside a pan of rice on the fire. Yo-Yo showed us around the truck, which was to be our home for the next month, and told us to always wash our hands in Dettol and rinse them in clean water before eating or handling food.

Shell-shocked, we retreated to the bar for a couple of beers to try to reorientate ourselves. What were we doing?

It was cold and wet and we were with a bunch of strangers on a camp site in Nairobi. We felt an uncomfortably long way from home.

After dinner, Yo-Yo announced that we all had duties to do: providing the wood for the fire, making sure there was enough food and water on the truck, loading and unloading the trailer. Katie and I were assigned water duty. It seemed simple enough. When we arrived at a new camp site, we'd get a hose and fill the water tanks so that we always had a good supply.

Our companions were an eclectic mix. There was an Irish science teacher, an English immigration officer, an Australian nurse, an Australian graphic designer, a Canadian geologist living in Malawi, a retired English lawyer from Eastbourne and a Danish man who worked in the postroom at the head office of Danish Railways. As we got to know them, it dawned on me just how confined our world in London had been. Neither of us had ever met such a variety of characters from such diverse worlds. Each of them fascinated us with tales from their own lives, whether it was about fake passports and customs scams, types of rock formation or Danish railway systems. It felt so good not to be talking about music and hype all the time.

We didn't sleep particularly well that night, having been told that we should be up for breakfast at seven and would be heading off by half past eight, and we woke in the worst of moods. We've never been at our most sociable in the morning, and are barely able to function until we've had a couple of cups of tea. On our first morning, breakfast had been cleared away early and by the time we crawled out of bed there was no tea left. We couldn't hide our displeasure and another pot was soon boiling just for us. We must have been a fearsome sight because it never happened again.

'The more you put into a trip like this,' Yo-Yo kept telling us all, 'the more you will get out of it!' It wasn't long before we had got the message. It was no good wishing that things were more comfortable or more organised; we just had to get on and deal with the way things were. It was our first lesson in adapting to our new lifestyle.

The group was split into three sub-groups with three people in each. Every third day our group was responsible for lunch, dinner and the following morning's breakfast. We were charged with the tasks of planning the meals and shopping for provisions in the markets as well as the actual cooking over the camp fire. The other two days we had free while the other groups took their turns.

Never ones to miss an opportunity, we quickly cornered the gentle-looking blond guy with a welcoming face and asked him if he would like to make up our group of three. An immigration officer from Jersey, John declared that he would love to join us (not that he was given much choice) but confessed that he couldn't cook.

'Don't worry,' we told him. 'Neither can we.'

He clearly didn't believe us – until it was our turn to cook.

We decided to keep things simple: baked potatoes in tin foil in the fire and marinated vegetables barbecued over the flame. How could it go so wrong? When we pulled the potatoes from the fire and undid the foil wrappings they were black, and the vegetables had shrunk to virtually nothing. There was no time to prepare anything else so our companions had to solemnly chew their way through our dreadful offerings, making polite noises about how delicious it was and how healthy carbon was to the digestive system.

We had to laugh. But if it hadn't been for John's steaks, which he had been cutting up with a penknife on the other side of the cooking tent, I'm not sure the others would have been as amused.

John had a dry sense of humour and, even more importantly, always made sure we had tea in the mornings. We discovered that he had been in the Territorial Army. 'Have you ever made anyone's chin wobble?' Katie asked. 'Barking orders at them?'

'Yes,' he admitted, which made us roar with laughter since we found him so easy to get on with. He laughed at us constantly, particularly when we were cooking, and we spent many nights together drinking too many beers and playing silly games. He was a good friend to us during that first month.

Those four weeks were everything we had hoped for. Every day was a new experience and we travelled through incredible landscapes. We shopped in local markets for food and slept under the stars. We learnt about the history and the culture of the areas we passed through, talking to everyone we came across about their lives. With each new person we got to know, we could feel ourselves changing. We remembered how to smile again – not the tight-lipped smiles of London but the beaming African smiles, all teeth and genuine happiness. We were getting life back into perspective. We no longer took water, food or shelter for granted and the beauty of the landscape continually took our breath away. As we drove through coffee plantations and avenues of Jacaranda trees with their purple flowers arching over the road to form a tunnel, Katie and I sat in the back of the truck, wearing Oakley sunglasses and Walkmans – really *listening* to music again as we watched the world go by. Every so often we would catch each other's eyes and smile. We felt so lucky. We began to remember who we were again. We laughed a lot and asked endless questions of everyone we met.

They say that you are never alone in Africa and we certainly found that to be true. Even when we camped in the middle of nowhere we would wake up to find local villagers staring at us curiously. It took us a while to get used to the fact that we were their entertainment – like their very own *Brookside*. Word would get around that there was something happening and the crowd of onlookers would gradually grow until Yo-Yo eventually felt the need to do a little juggling to give them their money's worth. The look of amazement on the children's faces as he showed off his talents was fabulous to behold. Yo-Yo had driven food into Bosnia during the war and while he was there he used to entertain the kids, in an attempt to give them some light relief from all the turmoil going on around them. He was extremely proficient at juggling, not only with brightly coloured balls – which had the African children wide eyed with amazement and delight – but also with flaming batons. People never eat outside in Africa, so we attracted attention just by doing that, but Yo-Yo's performances turned us into a travelling circus. The crowds would start by staring and end up shaking our hands and playing games with us.

That is not to say, however, that everything went according to plan during our first month of travelling. We drove north from Nairobi to Naivasha, Hell's Gate National Park, past Mount Kenya and into Sambura National Park, where our truck broke down. It had been growing steadily weaker for some time, black smoke billowing out behind us, until it finally ground to a halt in a small town.

Some of the group were very distressed at this unexpected interruption to our itinerary, but Katie and I could see no point in getting angry. All we could do was make the most of it, so we set about meeting as many people as possible and learning as much as we could about the area.

Chatting with two young boys, we were horrified to be told that the white man was closer to God.

'What do you mean?' I asked.

'First there is God,' one of them explained, 'then the white man and then the black man.'

We tried to tell them that we believed everyone was equal and that colour was irrelevant, but they were adamant and nothing we could say would change their minds.

We learnt how new-born babies are lifted up and faced towards Mount Kenya, and how all the houses and huts are built so that the front doors face the mountain. We learnt about tribes like the Kikuyu and the mighty warrior Samburus.

We also discovered that the British army were in town and we thought they could perhaps help us with the truck. As we sat by the side of the road, surrounded by curious locals, two uniformed soldiers walked past.

'They are from the Black Watch,' we were told. 'Training to go to Hong Kong for the handover. Tell us something we can say to them.'

Katie and I put on our best Scottish accents. 'Try, "Och aye the noo, have yer got any haggis?" '

The young Kenyans practised the phrase, not knowing what it meant, and parroted it out in perfect Scottish accents to the soldiers when they returned. Luckily, they saw the funny side.

Unfortunately, the mechanics in the camp didn't seem too keen on helping us, but they did diagnose the problem and we limped on in the hope of finding a garage.

We had lost a lot of time and were behind schedule now. When night fell we weren't in a safe area and had to seek out an enclosed cattle pen with armed guards for fear of the bandits lurking in the dark.

We were all slightly nervous and slept together in the cooking tent. Naturally, Katie and I were delighted to find ourselves sandwiched between two people who snored all night. On a midnight walk to the loo, we noticed that our armed guards were all fast asleep, dispelling any feeling of security which we might have had. Fortunately, we were too tired for our worries to keep us awake once we had sneaked back to our beds.

We were all so filthy when we finally reached Sambura National Park that the only thing any of us could think about was how to get clean.

'Why don't we build a shower?' John suggested. 'We could use river water and a sieve.'

The river water was rather a rich brown colour, which prompted me and Katie into making alternative plans. We hailed a tractor to take us to a game lodge and talked them into letting us have showers beside their extremely green swimming pool for $10 each. It was undoubtedly the most expensive shower I have ever taken, but also the best.

For four days and four nights Yo-Yo took the truck's engine to pieces and put it back together again. While he worked through the heat of the day we saw cheetahs, leopards, elephants, lions and buffalo. Katie and I had another go at cooking, producing a huge Spanish omelette that took an hour to cook, and corn on the cob that exploded like firecrackers when we put them in the camp fire. It was another disaster. We even tried to cook bananas, squidging chocolate buttons inside the skins. It was quite obvious that the local people thought we were mad.

What we couldn't understand was how the others managed to produce such wonderful meals. One guy would say, 'We're having Mexican tonight,' and then produce the whole works: fajitas, guacamole, tomato relishes, spices, sour cream. Or he'd say, 'Anybody want some pizza?' and just create one with no apparent effort at all.

We were four days behind schedule when we set off for the Ethiopian border. Yo-Yo's patience always amazed us. He had been up for four days and three nights trying to mend the truck's engine, using a small miner's torch strapped to his head and working until the batteries gave out. We would find him in the morning, still in his overalls, sitting in his driving seat because he was too tired to even go to bed. To make matters worse, during the day he had to contend with baboons and monkeys stealing his precious nuts and bolts. Now and again we would hear, 'You bastard!', and see a large stick flying through the air in the direction of a fleeing primate thief.

Although the civil war in Ethiopia finished in 1991, the border with Kenya is still a sensitive area due to landmines and bandits. The best way to cross is as quickly as possible as part of an armed convoy. We picked up three armed guards, one sitting in the front and the other two in the back with us, the barrels of their ancient guns waving in all directions as we bumped and swerved along the road. We asked politely if they would mind not pointing their weapons in our direction.

'It's OK,' one said, grinning. 'They're not loaded.'

The truck, which by now we had christened 'Bubble Trouble', didn't even make it to lunchtime before it shed a wheel and we wobbled to a halt. While Yo-Yo investigated the damage, we offered the guards egg mayonnaise and tomato and onion salad, which they stared at as if they had been delivered from Mars. Obviously deciding that our strange culinary offerings were better than nothing, they eventually ate what we laid in front of them and then left us in the middle of nowhere.

Somehow we managed to get the truck into the next small village in search of refuge for the night. We found it in the shape of a beautiful Italian mission, where Father José, a Mexican friar, allowed us to camp in his grounds. He wore a large sombrero and slouched around with his hands in his pockets like a gunslinger, calling out 'Hey, gringo' in his best spaghetti-Western fashion. The kids, all dressed in cast-off Versace and Armani T-shirts, had never seen anything like us before and just stared and giggled as we went about our nightly routines. Katie and I taught them how to play Grandmother's Footsteps.

It hadn't rained in the area for seven years, but Father José gave us some water. If people converted to Catholicism they were given an urn of water per family per day, but those who didn't weren't allowed any. We found this very distressing, particularly as Father José could often be seen watering his plants with a hose. Where, we wondered, was the Christianity in that?

Because water was in short supply and the jerrycans were so heavy, Katie and I decided to ration the water. Everybody was allowed some to wash with but when the Danish guy took a whole bucket to shave with, it was too much. To his fury I demanded the water back and gave him a small bowl instead, which he threw away in a tantrum. We had to laugh.

Our schedule slipped back another two days but we eventually arrived in Ethiopia. We had been expecting a famine-stricken disaster area but instead we found a green, pleasant land full of tall, slender, beautiful people. The Ethiopians are paler than their African neighbours and are very proud people with their own history, religion and language. In the Bible, Queen Bathsheba was said to have come from Ethiopia, and when she left Israel after having fallen in love with King Solomon, the son of David, she converted to believing that there was one God and brought the religion back. The claim is that the kings of Ethiopia can trace their ancestry back to King David. Ethiopian Orthodox is the main religion of the country and the church is very important in their society. The Ethiopian crosses, the rock churches cut straight from the stone, the beautiful priests, the monasteries, the murals, the paintings, the books, crowns and cloaks, some dating back to before the tenth century, all combine to create an aura of magic and mystery in the country. The curator of the National Museum in Addis Ababa explained to us that many of their national treasures have been taken out of the country but they are beginning to clamp down to protect what is left.

'Anything of real value that they find at the airport they will confiscate,' he explained. 'But a lot of it went out during the war, and in diplomatic bags.'

It is said that the Ark of the Covenant was brought to Ethiopia for safekeeping when the Muslims were attacking Israel several centuries ago and is still there. Apparently, only one priest is allowed to see it. He is chosen for the task when he is 30 years old and then has the responsibility for protecting it for the rest of his life. When he dies, the responsibility is passed on to another 30-year-old. It is said that all the priests given this task die from a cancer of the eye and many believe that the Ark comes from outer space and is radioactive. No-one but the priest is allowed to see it, in order to keep it from ever having any monetary or political value. Despite the fact that no-one has ever set eyes on it, everyone we talked to believed fervently that it was there and we were told, 'You should not doubt it.'

Ethiopia is one of only two African countries that was never really colonised. The Italians moved into Eritrea (then part of Ethiopia) because of its strategic position on the Red Sea, but the majority of the country remained independent. The Italians were only in Addis for about five years.

One of the things that we found really interesting is that Ethiopia has its own 24-hour clock which, for some unknown reason, starts at six in the morning. There are thirteen months in the year and they are currently in 1990. They celebrate Christmas on 7 January and Easter very soon after, meaning a month of almost permanent celebration.

The place amazed us. We had both been to developing countries before but had never come across such a giving culture. Instead of the children insisting 'Pen, give me pen', they would say, 'You have pen', and insist we take one. They would also give us nickel Ethiopian crosses. When we asked them how much, they would reply, 'Nothing. You just remember me.'

On one occasion while in a restaurant, two young women asked us to join them. We accepted their offer and they asked us what we wanted to eat. When the bill arrived, these complete strangers refused to let us pay as we were guests in their country. They then invited us to their house for coffee. Coffee drinking in Ethiopia is a ritual and if you accept you have to drink three cups. The first cup is to welcome you, the second is for happiness and the third is for marriage and children. We talked for ages until the older woman, a school teacher, had to go to work. Her companion then insisted we had coffee at *her* house – another three cups. It was also agreed that we would all meet up at seven o'clock – so that they could cook us dinner, we presumed.

We arrived on time that evening, clutching a local bottle of honey wine as our contribution. Immediately it became clear that we weren't expected. In fact, the younger woman seemed deeply embarrassed, and it wasn't until we realised that men wanting her services were beginning to arrive that we came to the conclusion that there had been some sort of misunderstanding. Now as embarrassed as they were, and assuming that nobody was interested in our honey wine, we left.

We told Yo-Yo of our strange experience.

'You weren't using Ethiopian time,' he explained. 'Seven o'clock here is actually one o'clock the next day. You were invited for lunch, not dinner!'

Oh, well, we'll know next time . . .

Amharic is the national language and very few people spoke English. The children would wave and smile, screaming, 'You, you, you, you,' which translated into 'How are you?' Remembering Yo-Yo's advice about the more you put in, the more you get out, we learnt a few phrases of Amharic and found that it worked a treat. To our astonishment, we were welcomed everywhere we dared to try them out. In a country that only five years before had been ravished by civil war, the people were the most hospitable we had ever met. Everywhere we looked we saw happy people who had virtually nothing.

Not that we walked about in a haze of happiness all the time. Although the monasteries we saw were amazing they did eventually become rather commonplace, until – and it sounds awful – AFM (Another Fucking Monastery) became part of our daily language.

Miraculously, we managed to reach Addis before the truck gave up completely. From there, in order to make up for lost time, Encounter Overland flew us to Bahar Dar, Gondar and Lalibella, each place more magical than the last. We flew in seventeen-seater propeller planes, taking off and landing at tiny airstrips with corrugated iron huts for terminal buildings. Katie had never particularly enjoyed flying and her first sight of one of the tiny, old, knackered planes didn't exactly boost her confidence. I, on the other hand, loved flying and know a little about the mechanics of how an aeroplane works. Pretending that I knew more than I actually did, I went through the science and physics of how flying worked to try to reassure her.

'The cockpit door is shaped like a coffin lid,' was her only comment once I had completed my morale-boosting lecture. I had to agree. But whatever I told her must have worked because we ended up taking four very bumpy

51

flights, one over the Simien Mountains where our left wing seemed to almost touch the peaks.

'Don't worry, sweetheart,' I reassured her as the rock face loomed threateningly outside the window. 'You'll be fine if you fly with me. I know I'm not going to die in a plane crash.'

We will always remember Ethiopia. Among many, many other things, we drank a lot of honey wine, bathed in hot springs, witnessed fantastic thunderstorms, sunrises and sunsets, watched dancers and listened to music. The best view of Lalibella, we discovered, was through a window in the smelliest toilet in town, and we met a politician in Gondar who explained to us that there was more gold and other natural resources in Ethiopia than in South Africa. He talked about corruption, foreign investment and the help needed to set the country straight. 'We need teachers and engineers,' he said, 'but no foreign company is allowed to own anything in Ethiopia. They can only lease from the government. To get the help we need, we have to bend the rules.'

We were walking into town for dinner as we chatted with him. Less than five minutes had gone by before there was a colossal clap of thunder, the heavens opened and the power went off in every house and shop. Never had we been caught in a storm of such force. We were soaked within seconds as the whole town rushed out around us, dancing in the streets and clapping and cheering. They hadn't seen rain for weeks and swept us along in their cele-brations.

Katie and Lizzie (left to right).

Robert Maxwell visits the original MTV Europe team, 1987.
(Lizzie; first row seated, third from left. Katie; first row standing, third from right)

Lizzie and Tina Turner.

Katie with Michael Jackson at Wembley.

A farewell family lunch, October 1996. (Lizzie and Katie; third and fourth from left)

Another world – at the source of the Blue Nile, Ethiopia, October 1996.

Eating indura, Ethiopia, November 1996.

The fateful descent of the Ethiopian Airways flight ET961, 23 November 1996.

The wreckage rests and tourists rush to rescue survivors.

The mangled carcass of the Boeing 767 (below and opposite).

Red Crescent workers deal with the tragic aftermath.

Comoros police and military examine the scene after the wreckage has been towed to shore.

© Popperfoto

Raindrops the size of pear drops jumped a foot in the air after hitting the dry ground, illuminated by the lightning. Looking to my left, I saw the rest of our group hiding from the rain in a doorway.

'Come on!' I shouted. 'It's fantastic out here.'

'We haven't got our raincoats,' one of them shouted back.

'So what?' I cried. 'It's not about trying to stay dry. Look! Everybody is celebrating.'

They wouldn't be persuaded so we left them behind and joined the street party.

Our only real problem on the trip was food, because we're both vegetarians. Wednesdays and Fridays were fine because they are fasting days and no meat is eaten – which meant there was an abundance of choice all around. Unfortunately, the rest of the week saw us having spaghetti and tomato sauce for every meal. The local dish, Indura, which is the staple diet of most Ethiopians, resembles a big, grey, soggy pancake. It's tasty now and then but not after three days on the run.

We never doubted that we had made the best decision of our lives. By the end of the first month, we were happier than we had ever been and were eager to get to India. Africa had whetted our appetites for everything that the world could offer us. We were also ready to go it alone. We had encountered problems in Africa but we had never felt afraid or worried. The unreliable truck had only added to the sense of adventure, spontaneity and camaraderie, landing us in places we would never otherwise have got to. We truly didn't miss London a bit. The trip was everything we had hoped for – and more. We were having a ball.

We had spoken to our families regularly, often from strange little telephone kiosks in the back of beyond, and sent numerous letters and postcards to friends. We had both written in-depth letters to our parents, crammed with details of all our experiences and our feelings about Ethiopia as we went along. We decided it would be appropriate to post them from Nairobi on our final day in Africa, so that they would have the complete story before we moved to the next continent. Katie had phoned her mum from Addis and explained that we were flying the next day and would call again from Nairobi.

We were so busy drinking in our surroundings that I never found a tranquil moment to read Carolyn's letter. I decided to wait until we got to India, where we would have more time to ourselves.

PART TWO
D-Day

KATIE

23 November 1996

Saying goodbye to our Encounter Overland group brought out mixed feelings in us. There's always a combination of sadness and nostalgia when something as brilliant as the month we'd just had ends. But then Lizzie and I were so excited about the next stage of our journey that we could hardly wait to get going. We felt ready to move on; ready to be truly independent. Some of our travelling companions had already gone their own ways, so we said goodbye to the others and headed to the airport with Yo-Yo.

We were looking forward to getting back to Nairobi, not least because we had a whole new wardrobe of clothes in the rucksack we had left there a month earlier. Never before had I been so excited about the prospect of a change of clothing – the thought of a clean, new T-shirt was almost too luxurious to contemplate. We had begun to treasure small luxuries like this.

We had also left the majority of our money at the lock-up and, however much our lifestyles had changed, we were looking forward to having some cash again. We had miscalculated our funds for Ethiopia and only taken $200 between us for a month, which was nowhere near enough, even though Encounter Overland had covered all food, accommodation, entry fees to game parks and the emergency flight tickets we'd had to buy. Thankfully, John had been very understanding and lent us enough to get us through, trusting us to send him a cheque at some point.

In Addis we had arranged to meet 'the Flying Spanner', a mechanic who Encounter Overland had sent out to help Yo-Yo with the truck. He was an extremely tall Scotsman with a wry sense of humour, and spent his entire life flying to the rescue of stranded groups of travellers. We clicked with him immediately and, since he was flying to Nairobi the next day, had arranged to meet up with him there too.

We planned to spend two days in Nairobi, which would give us time to get all our laundry done so that we could start afresh in India. We had already planned to meet Charlie in Bombay and needed to confirm our tickets. I couldn't wait to see him. I was itching to tell him everything about our trip so far and was really looking forward to spending some time with him again.

On our last night in Addis Ababa we had a long conversation with a CID officer. He had arrived a day early and was part of the next group that Yo-Yo was to take around Ethiopia. He was about 45 and travelling alone. We talked extensively and enthusiastically about how wonderful the trip was. We were intrigued by his job and eventually got on to the topic of psychos.

'Can you spot a psycho in a crowd?' I asked.

'Yes,' he said, confidently. 'There's something about the look in their eyes and their mannerisms.'

'I bet they'd be acting weird and making themselves noticeable,' I agreed, cockily.

'That doesn't tend to be the case,' he argued gently. 'They often appear quite quiet and unassuming.'

It was a conversation which we never imagined would have an impact on our lives. We were just passing the time with a congenial stranger, and he was simply one of the many people we were meeting all the time, teaching us about other walks of life. We never thought for one moment that his words would become so important to us.

When we arrived at Addis Ababa International Airport we simply stared, aghast at what awaited us inside the terminal. To say the airport was busy would be something of an understatement. It heaved under an unbelievable chaos of sweating human bodies and piles of luggage. It would have been like an ant hill, but ants are much more organised and able to move around to get about their business. This was a gridlock of hot human flesh made anxious by its own confusion. It was impossible to see where the queues for checking in started or finished. If we had hung back politely until it was our turn, we would have been there forever.

'We're going to have to be assertive here,' Lizzie said, swinging her rucksack on to her back.

'We'll check in and then come back for a farewell coffee,' I told Yo-Yo, before turning to follow my friend into battle.

To add to our discomfort, we were wearing jeans, fleeces and boots because with just one rucksack between us we were very limited for space. We also had a day pack and a plastic bag that had definitely seen better days, containing our very small sleeping bags.

With the rucksack swinging back and forth like a punch-bag and our elbows digging and gouging at the mass of bodies in front of us, we forced our way through the crowd like explorers hacking their way through primary jungle.

'Excuse me! Sorry! Oops! Thank you so much!' We pushed ourselves forward, smiling as sweetly as we could at everyone we banged into. We emerged, glowing and triumphant, at the check-in desk for Ethiopian Airways, flight ET961. We grinned at each other in mutual admiration and fumbled for our passports and tickets, which were already beginning to take on the soiled, crumpled look of veteran travellers.

The tickets were originally dated for 24 November. However, since we had ended up flying internally around Ethiopia, arriving back at Addis Ababa earlier than originally scheduled, we had decided to bring our flight forward and give ourselves more time in Nairobi. We had wanted to fly even earlier but the only seats available were for Saturday 23 November. Our tickets had been stickered with the change of date without any fuss.

Slapping the papers down on the desk, we smiled triumphantly at the woman sitting opposite, who appeared puzzled as to why we were quite so pleased with ourselves. 'Smoking or non-smoking?' she enquired, with well trained, automatic charm.

For the last month, we had been promising each other that we would give up smoking. We hadn't quite found the right moment to make the final effort but we were determined that we would as soon as we reached India. Having said that, neither of us liked sitting in the smoking area on flights.

'I only like the smell of my own smoke,' Lizzie always said. 'And although I'm willing to kill myself, I don't want any help from anyone else.'

I had a different reason. I always preferred to sit in front of the wings because it's less turbulent than the back of the plane, which seems to be where the smokers are always sent.

This time, however, when we were asked for our preference, we didn't answer immediately. We looked at each other in silence, as if it might be a trick question, then back to the bemused woman in a synchronised double take. Then we blurted out simultaneously, 'Smoking, please,' as if our lives depended on it. There is no explanation for our decision, unless we both saw it as a last chance to enjoy tobacco before giving up in India. Or perhaps it was some sort of divine intervention on our behalves. We will never know. Our boarding passes were issued and we watched our large rucksack disappear along the conveyor belt into the bowels of Addis Airport. Next time we saw it, we would be back in Nairobi.

Turning round, we took another deep breath and plunged back into the seething mob, making our way over to the exit door where Yo-Yo was patiently waiting for his farewell cup of coffee. Breathless from the exertions of just moving through the human mire, we had just reached the door when an armed guard stepped in front of me, barring my exit, and jabbered something at me in Amharic. Even if there were any words that I recognised, he spoke far too fast for me to catch them. His face was fixed in a mask of grim determination.

'I don't understand.' I shook my head, assuming I had done something terribly wrong; my heart was beating and blood rushing to my face at the possibility of an embarrassing scene in a language I didn't understand. He repeated whatever he had said before, but louder, so I said, 'I don't understand' louder. We both became frustrated and Lizzie started giggling nervously.

Two Israeli guys were now trying to get into the airport, their way blocked by me and the guard. 'He says it's impossible for you to go back out,' one of them translated for us.

'Why?' I asked indignantly, but they just shrugged. They were in their early twenties and looked like they were travellers. One was fair and the other dark, and they both had friendly faces.

It was obvious the guard wasn't going to change his mind and any argument would have been futile, so we had to catch Yo-Yo's attention through the window and say our goodbyes with dramatic waves and the blowing of passionate kisses. Sadly, we watched him walk away.

'What next, then?' I asked Lizzie.

'Immigration, I guess,' she replied. 'We have to fill out these forms.'

We started filling out the forms which we had watched people handing over at every airport we had been to. They nearly always have to be corrected by the immigration officers, thereby holding up the queues at every possible stage.

'These forms are simple,' I declared as we ticked and scribbled. 'I can't see why they cause everyone such problems.'

'People just don't read them properly,' Lizzie said. 'If they did, there wouldn't be all these hold-ups.'

Twenty-five minutes later, after the officer had re-filled in both our forms and corrected all the mistakes, we were finally allowed through to customs. Our tickets and passports were checked for the third time and finally stamped. Everywhere we turned there were more security men for us to get past, but since half the guards had looked at our passports upside down we didn't feel that the numbers signified efficiency. If a terrorist was stopped by this lot, it would be more by luck than judgement, we joked.

While I'm not a fan of flying, I've always loved departure lounges. At least, I love Heathrow and the other European airports I've been through on business. Duty free shops are such wonderful places in which to spend money. After a month of sitting in an uncomfortable van and roughing it on camp sites, we felt ready for a bit of luxury: inhaling perfumes, fingering silk scarves, trying moisturiser samples, ogling exotic bottles of booze, comparing the merits of different vitamin pills. I bounded up the stairs two at a time in eager anticipation of the heady delights await- ing us, ready to spend what was left of our first month's money.

As I reached the top step I came to a sudden horrified halt and Lizzie smacked into my back, sending me hurtling forward. We both stared, slack-jawed with shock. There was one little shop – more of a booth, really – with a single bottle of Blue Stratos gathering dust in the window. Even that had to be bought in American dollars, which we didn't have spare.

We were hugely disappointed; bereft at the lack of shop- ping opportunities. I was so desperate to spend that I tried to swap my Ethiopian currency – about £10 worth – for dollars at the Bureau de Change, but they refused. They were happy to take dollars and turn them into local currency but were not the slightest bit interested in chang- ing them back.

I shouted over to Lizzie that it was no good. Feeling really despondent now, the only thing that cheered me up was seeing the friendly-faced Israelis again and we exchanged smiles of recognition. I walked back to Lizzie, frustrated at not being able to spend our money.

'I've got to spend some money,' I wailed plaintively.

'Let's eat,' Lizzie suggested. 'That'll cheer us up.'

The food counter, the only place we could possibly part

with our cash, was selling so little worth eating that I had to order an omelette, despite my aversion to eggs. Lizzie just ordered a cup of coffee.

Once we had come to terms with our disappointment, we sipped our coffee and looked around to see what was going on. The two Israeli guys walked past.

'They're rather cute,' Lizzie said wistfully.

'Funny you should say that. I was just thinking the same thing,' I agreed.

We both giggled girlishly.

*

Despite being an international airport, the departure lounge in Addis left a lot to be desired. It was one big, grey, square room with rows of hard plastic seats, and hordes of people were just sitting around, waiting for something to happen. There was a stifling air of boredom and frustration.

The last mouthful of omelette was just sliding down my throat when an official came over to us.

'You must make your way over to the gate,' he told us, which was surprising since there was still an hour and a half until take-off, but we assumed there must be a reason and did as he suggested.

We reached another level of security and had to walk through a metal detector. I got there first and strolled through without eliciting so much as a squeak from the bleepers. Lizzie, on the other hand, set them all off and seemed to put the whole airport on red alert.

'It's your boots,' the security officer said, waving imperiously at Lizzie's feet, which were identically shod to mine. She took them off and tried again, but the same thing happened.

'Necklace.' He pointed to the Ethiopian cross around her neck, which was also the same as mine. She obediently took it off and handed it over but to no avail. They decided to search her instead and confiscated her matches, assuring her they would return them on landing.

'I bet that's ours,' I said to Lizzie, pointing to the right-hand plane, as we looked out of the huge window once we'd finally been allowed through. We plonked ourselves down in some seats in the sun and watched it being prepared for take-off, trying to see if we could spot our luggage being loaded on. It was a beautiful day and, as the sun streamed in through the window, I didn't feel at all nervous about flying. After all those little propeller-driven tin buckets in Ethiopia this was going to be a breeze; a big, shiny, new plane glistening in the morning sunlight.

Despite the tedium of having to hang around an airport for hours, our spirits were sky high again. We were never down for long because we were both so conscious of what we were doing and how important it was to appreciate every moment. We almost needed to pinch ourselves to check we weren't dreaming.

'I can't believe we've only got eleven months left,' I said, genuinely concerned all of a sudden. 'I'm worried it isn't going to be enough.'

'You've only had a month,' Lizzie tried to reason with me. 'Don't start worrying about when it will finish just yet.'

'I know, but I'm worried it's all going to go too quickly,' I explained. 'Maybe we should go on to South America after we've done the States. And we should come back to Africa before we come home – it's an amazing place and we've only scratched the surface. There's much more that we need to explore. I can even imagine living here. Since were already travelling we might as well keep going and get it all out of our systems before we go home, get married, live in the country and start families.'

I poured all these feelings out so quickly, one after the other, that Lizzie laughed. But I knew she could see the logic in what I was saying.

We both fell into deep thought for a while as the gate filled up around us. I began thinking about how much our lives had already changed. I looked across at Lizzie in her once white, now grey, T-shirt, and wondered what had possessed her to buy white for a trip like this. But that's Lizzie. She has always considered herself to be sensible and rational when in fact she's barking mad. We all call her Mrs Malaprop because she constantly uses the wrong words to describe things. She's also an expert at stating the obvious. If the temperature's well past 90 degrees in the shade, she'll be the one to say, 'It's really hot today.'

At the moment in the airport she looked very relaxed and happy, a long way from the stressed-out, tired, over-worked, dissatisfied person she had been just two months earlier. I was so happy to be travelling with her – my best friend.

I reflected on all the stuff we had been through over the years: some happy, some sad, but everything shared. She was always so sympathetic about break-ups with boyfriends, with tons of good advice for every possible trauma. As a friend she would give everything she had and nothing was ever too much trouble. The funny thing about her is that she lacks confidence in herself, which is strange considering she is always successful at everything she does, whether it be her job, sailing her father's boat or learning to scuba dive. She has a fantastic determination to do things well if she is going to do them at all. In fact, the only thing I can remember her being unsuccessful at was her desire to have green fingers – but at least her withered plants gave us a laugh.

I could hardly believe that the same person who was so at home driving flashy cars around London was now crumpled and travel stained and didn't care how she looked. But then, Lizzie can adapt to any situation with chameleon-like ease. I was tremendously impressed by her when she took her new job at London Records without any apparent fear, and how she seemed to cope for all the family when her sister died. She is never afraid to show her emotions in any situation and has a genuineness which people respect. During that first month away, I witnessed how adept she was at interacting with different people and making them feel relaxed in her presence. I always think that friends represent you to others when you are not around and I can't think of anyone I would rather be represented by.

I have never been able to understand why some people claim to find Lizzie intimidating when they first meet her. We have grown so close over the years that we hardly even need to talk, and are able to communicate with a sort of sign language of our own. We can be at opposite sides of a crowded room and Lizzie will throw me a look that will perfectly express what I'm thinking. Not surprisingly, this communicating skill has got us into trouble on occasion when those around us have assumed we're laughing at them. We rarely argue, and if we do, we can't keep it up for very long. It always seems unnatural and we end up laughing.

The minutes ticked by slowly in the airport, so we started to play one of our favourite games: making up life scenarios for the people sitting around us.

'I bet that woman is a missionary,' Lizzie said.

'Why do you say that?' I asked.

'Well, she's white, elderly and travelling alone.'

'Oh. Do you think if Margaret Thatcher was travelling on her own people who didn't know her would think she was a missionary?' She grinned. 'Look at that poor bloke in the neck brace,' I continued. 'I wonder how he did that. It looks painful.'

'See that man with the children?' Lizzie nodded towards a Kenyan in his late thirties with three beautiful children. 'I bet they're flying to Nairobi to be met by their mother.'

The eldest, a little girl of about seven with beautifully

braided hair, dressed in pink leggings and a Mickey Mouse T-shirt, started to play peek-a-boo with us. She had one of those genuine, life-enhancing smiles that we had seen all over Ethiopia and Kenya. The middle one was about four and he had the same wonderful smile as his sister as he played with his dad. It looked as if he was wearing his best outfit, his shirt and trousers giving him the appearance of a miniature grown-up. The youngest was still a babe in arms.

They had been visiting relatives in Ethiopia, we decided, and were now on their way home.

The father looked affluent, a professional of some sort, dressed in casual trousers and shirt like his son. He watched his children proudly as they played together quietly.

A group of Israeli businessmen took the seats next to us just as we decided we were in dire need of cigarettes. They were dressed quite formally, although not wearing suits, and some had grey hair. We guessed they were in their early forties. I noticed that one of them had tasselled slip-on leather shoes over white socks, two of my pet hates. We assumed they were businessmen since they didn't appear to be on holiday and one or two of them had briefcases. They were chatting and laughing among themselves as they waited.

'Would you watch our bags for us while we nip out for a cigarette?' I asked the men.

'Of course,' one of them replied. 'But what if we find all your money?'

'No chance – it's too well hidden,' I joked.

Little did they know that we were virtually penniless and eager to get to our funds in Nairobi.

It took a while to find anyone with a light since all our matches had been confiscated, so we only had time for a couple of puffs before we noticed people gathering themselves together and moving towards the door leading to the plane. We rushed back to our belongings.

'We didn't find the money,' the same Israeli said, grinning.

'We told you. You were looking in the wrong place,' Lizzie retorted.

Our banter was cut short as officials began to herd us towards the plane on the left-hand side. We were surprised, having convinced ourselves that the right-hand one was ours.

As we made our way on to it, I noticed an unusual number of mechanics and cleaners in white overalls coming on and off around us. 'Why are there so many maintenance people around?' I asked Lizzie, waiting for her to give some logical answer.

'The drains are probably blocked,' she joked. 'I expect they're unblocking the sewage pipes to make sure the toilets don't overflow during the flight.'

Happy to accept that as being as likely as any other explanation, I laughed and we stepped on board to be greeted by a stunningly beautiful stewardess, whose uniform of an oversized white cotton dress with red, yellow and green striped borders was very similar to the Ethiopian national dress. It was pulled in around her waist with a sash in the same colours. It reached almost to the floor, with long sleeves. We had been thinking about buying them for ourselves in Ethiopia, but due to our miscalculations over the funds hadn't been able to afford them. She smiled, looked at our tickets and motioned for us to go to the back of the plane with all the other smokers. Being a 767, the aisle seemed to go on forever as we searched out seats D and E in row 33.

The seating was divided into three sections with two seats at either window and three in the middle. Ours were on the right of the middle block in the second to last row. The two Israeli travellers we'd last seen in the departure lounge were at the front of the economy section and as we made our way along we passed people we had made up life stories about as they rummaged around in overhead lockers and settled into their seats.

The plane appeared to be relatively new. We were among the last to board and most of the passengers were already in their seats. The flight seemed to be full.

An Ethiopian man was sitting in Lizzie's seat in the middle and we asked if he would mind moving to the aisle so that we could sit together. He readily agreed but seemed rather nervous and ill at ease.

*

As we made ourselves comfortable and strapped ourselves in, the man began fiddling with his seatbelt as if he didn't know what to do with it. He watched us fasten

71

ours and then did the same. This was obviously his first-ever flight. Once he had mastered the seatbelt, he started exploring the ashtray, opening and closing it over and over again, and then moved on to the contents of his seat pocket, pulling out each item, studying it closely without reading it and then putting it back. He tried on his head-phones and we pulled out our in-flight magazines in an attempt to block him out of our minds. He was becoming a little irritating.

In one of the magazines we came across a recipe for Indura, a dish we were both heartily sick of and hoped not to have to try again for a very long time. The taste is sour because of whatever grain they use to make it but appar-ently it's remarkably nutritious. The base for any meal served in Ethiopia, it doubles up as a fork because you pick the meat and vegetables up with it. We concentrated hard on the words to distract ourselves from everything going on around us – so much so that neither of us noticed the safety procedures being shown. Suddenly, we were taxiing down the runway in preparation for take-off.

We got into the air without any problem and once the plane had levelled out, I relaxed and looked around. To my left I could see the Kenyan family with the little girl in pink. The father was holding the baby on his lap while the other two were messing around next to him.

'Ding!' The no-smoking went off and we were able to have our first in-flight cigarette.

Being more nervous than Lizzie when it comes to flying, I tend to look around me and keep a check on what's happening. She can switch off and concentrate on her book or whatever she is doing. After about twenty minutes, the stewardesses began routinely wheeling the drinks trolleys up the aisles. Lizzie was still buried in the magazine, obviously trying to memorise the recipe for Indura. God knows when she was thinking she would make it.

As I idly watched them work, the stewardesses suddenly wheeled the trolleys back with unnatural speed. I sensed a tension in their movements and expressions.

'Lizzie.' I nudged her. 'I think there's something going on on this flight.'

Lizzie looked up from her magazine, more than used to me thinking something is wrong on a flight. She looked down the aisle to where people were moving around. 'Probably someone hyperventilating,' she suggested calmly. She watched the goings on for a few more moments, intrigued despite herself, and then went back to her reading.

Whatever it was that was happening, we couldn't see it because it wasn't taking place in our part of the plane. We could only see as far as the galley ahead, which was about twenty rows in front of us. There didn't appear to be an unusual amount of noise or people rushing about. Apart from the looks on the stewardesses' faces, nothing seemed particularly out of the ordinary. I'm not sure anyone else had even noticed the tension.

Although willing to accept Lizzie's explanation as a possibility, I wasn't quite able to dismiss the scene as if it wasn't happening. I kept watching. One of the stewardesses walked hurriedly down the aisle to our left and disappeared into the galley behind us. It looked to me as if she was almost crying. 'I don't know,' she was saying. 'I don't know but he has something in his hand.'

I instinctively knew there was a bomb on board and that all my worst nightmares were about to come true. Taking a deep breath, I forced down the urge to scream and fall to pieces. I nudged Lizzie again and told her what I had just heard the stewardess say. 'There's something serious happening on this plane,' I said, my voice wobbly. I don't know how but I just knew I was right.

I was desperate to make her engage with what I now felt to be a life-threatening situation. In a split second everything had been turned upside down. Euphoria and serenity had been replaced with alarm and confusion. I had no proof that there was anything untoward happening but a sixth sense told me this was serious. I felt terrified and over-whelmed, helpless and vulnerable, charged and waiting for an imminent explosion. Fuck, was all I could think. We're going to get blown up.

Adrenalin must have been pumping through me and I could feel my hands growing clammy. I knew I had to suppress my emotions and not give way to panic – in the back of my mind I knew I *could* be wrong – but it was taking all my strength.

As I looked around the cabin I could see that other people were beginning to show signs of unease. A group of passengers on the right-hand aisle started moving about, some laughing and some looking back towards us over their shoulders like frightened, naughty schoolchildren.

Maybe they know something I don't, I thought, because they can see further up the plane. But they didn't look any less confused than I felt.

So many times in the past Lizzie had been able to allay my fears with her simple or jokey explanations for every bump or thump, but this time I knew she wouldn't have a ready answer.

'No, there isn't,' was all she could think to say, and I could tell she was nervous too. 'I didn't hear the stewardess say that.'

'Well, I did,' I said matter of factly. 'There's a bomb on this plane.' I was on the verge of becoming overwhelmed by panic again.

I had said the word 'bomb' and there was no taking it back. I was immediately 100 per cent sure that I was right. Until that moment I had allowed a tiny chink of my mind to believe that I was being stupid and imagining the whole thing. Not any more. We sat in silence for what seemed like an eternity, waiting to find out what was going on and hoping beyond hope that some rational and logical explanation would be forthcoming.

It can't have been more than two minutes before all our worst fears were confirmed. A man's voice came over the tannoy, speaking in Amharic. We had no way of knowing who he was. He might have been the captain, for all we knew. The message was then repeated in French. Although I don't speak Amharic and only have schoolgirl French, the word 'bomba' rang loud and clear out of the jumble of foreign words and static. I knew exactly what was being said and I didn't want to hear it. I blocked my ears and started to sing opera.

'Shut up!' Lizzie snapped, trying to listen to the voice.

'I know what he's saying,' I protested, 'and we don't need to hear it!'

The more I tried to block the voice out, the louder and more vivid it seemed to become, ringing in my ears and taunting me with the news that I was about to suffer the most terrifying ordeal of my life and there was nothing that I could do to escape it. So often I would want to hear something desperately and then miss it at the last minute or it would be drowned by the smallest rustle of someone's newspaper, but these words wouldn't let my attention slip, wouldn't allow me to think about anything else, would not leave me alone. It's usually almost impossible to hear what someone is saying over an in-flight tannoy even when it's in your own language, but this time the man might just as well have been sitting in the seat next to me with a megaphone. There was absolutely no room for doubt left in my mind.

Eventually the disembodied voice spoke in English, but by then I didn't need any translation. 'We have hijacked this plane,' he announced, 'and we have a bomb. We don't want to use the bomb but we will, so it is very important that you do what we say. Meanwhile, we are re-directing this flight.'

The announcement had lasted about ten seconds and

had contained six short pieces of information. It made our situation very clear to us but it didn't seem enough to justify the feelings which it produced inside us. I could see that everyone else was undergoing the same emotional process as me. The whole plane was in shock.

As the realisation began to sink in, people started getting out of their seats and looking up the plane, obviously trying to work out what was going on. Suddenly a man in his mid-twenties appeared at the front of our section, screaming and motioning for everyone to sit down. He looked like an Ethiopian and it was obvious that he was part of whatever was going on. He didn't appear to be armed but he had authority and everyone sat back down immediately. Within five seconds he had disappeared again, heading up to the front of the plane.

My mind was whirling as it tried to work out what to do with the information it was receiving. The adrenalin was pumping through my body and I was fighting to remain on top of it and not allow panic to sweep me away into hysteria. I had to somehow stay in control of myself.

'I want to get off,' I told Lizzie in a quiet little voice.

'I know, sweetheart,' she replied in a deadpan monotone, 'but we can't.'

Then we both sat very still, staring forward, waiting for the first signs of the explosion which now seemed inevitable.

My rising panic must have been obvious for all to see, my face set in a mask of terror, because a man sitting across the aisle from me said, 'It is time to pray.'

I now felt annoyed and distressed at the same time. 'I know,' I snapped.

He was obviously trying to help but I didn't want to engage in conversation with anyone while my brain was still trying to take in what was happening. I wanted to be having a beer in a bar somewhere in Nairobi with Lizzie and the Flying Spanner. Instead, I was 37,000 feet in the air, facing imminent death. A faceless voice had turned our lives upside down and I didn't want anyone else invading what little space I had left on the aeroplane. I needed a moment to readjust to a new, horrific reality.

Lizzie put her arms around me as if to defend me from attack. 'She knows,' she told him, and the man returned to his own thoughts.

We sat back in our seats, clinging together for support, as if trying to suck up any surplus mental strength that might be flying around in the air. We stayed silent for a long time and eventually Lizzie spoke.

'We have to accept our situation and deal with it,' she said. 'It will probably be OK. Pilots aren't trained to be heroes. He'll just do whatever the hijackers want. So although it will be horrible for a while, we *will* be OK.' I could tell from the way she spoke, and from the look on her face, that she was trying to reason with herself as much as with me.

I joined in her thought processes, determined to keep my potential panic suppressed. 'If this was a Lockerbie-type bomb, we'd all be dead and we'd have known nothing about it. We must have some negotiating value to these people. We must be worth more to them alive than dead or they would have just killed us.'

The amazing thing about the human brain is that it can adjust to deal with almost anything. If I had been told what was going to happen on that flight in advance, I would have thought I'd have fallen to pieces, unable to cope with the pressure. I would have expected to become hysterical and simply break down. But that didn't happen. I certainly didn't feel OK, but to my surprise I found that I could deal with what was going on. Lizzie was the same. It was as if our brains had rationalised what was likely to happen and found a way for us to handle the pressure.

Most hijacking situations, we reminded ourselves, do get resolved peacefully. Most hijackers are 'professionals' with a cause, however obscure, and ours were unlikely to be any different. The chances were they would have a goal which they were aiming for and, providing they were able to achieve it, or at least a negotiable part of it, it would all work out. It sounds bizarre now, but we rationally decided that the most likely scenario would be that we would be taken to a runway somewhere and be kept prisoner for a few days while the powers that be negotiated our release. They might even let the women and children go. The worst outcome we could envisage was that a couple of us might be shot in the course of some SAS-type rescue on the plane. Somehow those odds didn't seem too terrifying compared to the possibility of a bomb on board.

*

In search of more information and hope, we turned to a map of the world in the airline magazine and looked up the trouble spots to see which ones were within flying distance of Ethiopia.

'We could be going to Chad,' we reasoned, 'Or Zaire or Pakistan.' Lizzie then looked up information on the plane itself and worked out that on a full tank of fuel the 767 could fly for eight hours. We had taken off at eleven o'clock and we hadn't yet been in the air for an hour. This ordeal might last for another seven hours, and then it would all be over.

We weren't the only ones being amazingly calm at this stage. Even the children weren't crying, which shows how tranquil and untroubling the atmosphere in the cabin must have seemed to them. A strange feeling of camaraderie sprung up. We were all in this together and so the barriers which we automatically put up when we are travelling in close confinement with strangers were dropping. We had something in common and we needed to share our feelings with those around us, albeit without many words.

There were a number of theories going around as to where we might be going. 'Given the position of the sun, and given that we are still over the sea, I would say we are heading for Madagascar,' said a Swiss man behind us. He was a large man with grey, receding hair and a beard. He then handed us a container of water which made me surprisingly nervous.

I instinctively felt that we should be behaving as discreetly and inconspicuously as possible. I didn't think we should be doing anything unless we were told to by the hijackers themselves. Were we allowed to drink? We had no idea and I didn't want this man drawing attention to us in this way.

'Where did you get that?' I asked him.

'There is plenty more where that came from,' he said.

'If you know where to look.' His supercilious smile and blasé attitude seemed completely inappropriate to me. Surely the hijackers would be nervous and any wrong move on our behalf could make them angry and panic them into some rash action? We had no idea who this man was and, given his confident smile, it occurred to both Lizzie and me that he might be one of the hijackers, or at least in league with them in some way. He seemed surprisingly cool given the situation, as was his younger companion, by his side.

Everyone was undoubtedly as thirsty and shocked as we were, so it was unfair that they couldn't have a drink. We were grateful for the man's gesture, but it frightened us and seemed wrong. Perhaps his smiley face was trying to instil confidence in us, but it was having the opposite effect.

The air stewardesses sat quietly in their seats behind us. It seemed that no-one could tell us any more than the information the disembodied voice had given us. It was clear that nobody knew the rules of the dangerous game we were being forced to play and just taking a glass of water seemed an unacceptable risk.

'Do you think our parents know this is going on?' I

suddenly asked Lizzie. I couldn't bear the thought of them fearing for my life.

'No,' Lizzie said. 'This sort of thing probably happens all the time in this part of the world. I doubt if it will make the news in England.'

'When we get to a runway and they let us go,' I remember saying after a few moments' thought, 'I'll need to get my bag from the overhead locker.'

'We won't have time for anything like that,' Lizzie said. 'We'll probably have to leave everything.'

I felt a surge of panic and fought back the tears. 'I have to have it,' I said, my voice choking in my throat. 'It's got my address book in and my whole family has moved so I don't know any of their phone numbers by heart. Without it I won't be able to contact anyone.'

'OK, I see your point. We'll get it when the time comes,' she replied.

We fell silent for a while and then began to talk about how we were looking forward to being on the ground in Nairobi, having a couple of beers and writing home about our latest adventure. We knew it was important to keep our minds positive and focus on what would happen once we were released, to reconfirm in our minds that we would be OK. We deliberately imagined scenarios in the future when our horrific ordeal would be behind us. Nothing was happening and we didn't want to become locked into our terror. We talked about the places we were going to visit and considered it quite possible that we would still get to Nairobi in time to meet the Flying

Spanner the following night. We managed to keep this up for about an hour.

Eventually, we began to run out of words. Since we had managed to give ourselves a temporary false sense of security, I decided to distract myself and got out my book, *Masai Dreaming*, while Lizzie delved into *I Dreamed of Africa*.

We immersed ourselves in our reading with great concentration. I was quite near the end of my book and I noticed an Italian guy looking over my shoulder. I could feel that he was willing me to finish so that he could ask to borrow it to give himself something to do. It seems inconceivable that I was able to read a book under such circumstances, but at the time it was the natural thing to do.

Never had either of us been so frightened or tense – yet we weren't smoking. My mouth felt very dry, making the idea of smoke unappealing, but it also seemed rather a foolish and trivial vice compared to what was happening to us. We were both searching inside ourselves for something a little more powerful than tobacco.

*

The stewardesses began handing out meals to the children, after one of the crew had received permission to do so. It was a hopeful sign and gave us a great deal of confidence. If the hijackers had the compassion to think of the children, they couldn't be complete monsters.

When the food was handed out, we'd been in the air for

about three hours. With a wave of horror, I realised that I needed to go to the toilet. The idea of standing up and making myself conspicuous to whoever was watching the cabin absolutely terrified me. As long as we stayed small and invisible in our seats, giving no-one any cause for concern, I felt we had a strong chance of survival. To stand up and walk out into the aisle where anyone could shoot me was almost more than I could bear to contemplate. The only option, however, was to wet myself where I sat, but at the back of my mind I knew we could be on the plane for days.

Now that I was aware of my bladder, the pain began to increase, and the waves of panic sweeping through me made me feel faint and nauseous at the same time.

Were we allowed to just get up and wander to the toilet? Would they shoot anyone who seemed to be making trouble? It seemed utterly unreal that I was having to ask myself these questions.

'I've got to go to the loo!' I hissed at Lizzie.

'Oh, God!' The news obviously appalled her too. 'Is that wise?'

'I've got to brave it. I can't hold on any longer.' I was determined now.

I rose to my feet. I tried to keep myself small by bending down as far as seemed reasonable, but I didn't want to look as if I was trying to escape either so I moved hurriedly to the back of the plane with my heart crashing in my ears. The toilet was only about six feet away from us but it was the longest walk of my life. I felt sure that every eye in the cabin was fixed on me and that at any moment there would be a shout followed by a shot. Terror must have been written all over my face because one of the stewardesses sitting at the back made a calming motion with her hands and smiled. I can't be doing anything too criminal, I decided.

When I pressed the flush, the explosion of water into the bowl made me jump out of my skin – for a split second, I thought the bomb had gone off. Then, when I realised it was just the air being sucked down the toilet, I convinced myself that the hijackers would have heard the noise from the front of the plane and were on their way to investigate.

Mustering up all my courage, I poked my nose back outside the door. All was as quiet as before and eventually I sank back into my seat and felt a wave of relief, both from the physical pain of a full bladder and the emotional pressures of so much fear. Now we could disappear back into invisibility and let the situation evolve around us.

'I've got to go now,' Lizzie said, and I felt every nerve and muscle in my body seize up with tension again. Taking a deep breath, she stood up and made her way to the back of the plane. It seemed like an age before I saw her emerge from the cubicle and walk back towards me. Once the ordeal was over we actually felt comparatively relaxed, and we struck up a conversation with the Ethiopian man sitting next to us, who was reading the Bible.

We knew he spoke Amharic and asked him for a more accurate translation of what had been said over the tannoy and what he thought it all meant.

'They said they were anti-government,' he told us, 'so if all they want is political asylum we'll be OK. But if they are anything to do with the vice-president we are in trouble.'

We had heard a lot about the vice-president and how he had recently been sent to prison for alleged fraud. It seemed quite likely that Ethiopia's recent history of dictatorships and corruption might have something to do with the hijackers' demands.

Our neighbour told us he was a gynaecologist. 'I am on my way to Kenya. I want to increase my knowledge and take what I learn back to Ethiopia.' He confessed, as we had already guessed, that he had never been on a plane before and had never actually been outside the borders of his own country. He was about 40 years old and gentle looking. He had a colleague with him who was sitting further up the plane and he would occasionally walk back to check he was OK. He didn't appear to be overly concerned with the situation, which gave us confidence.

*

I looked across at the Kenyan family. The father had the baby on his knee and was feeding him a blackcurrant drink from a bottle. The two older children were asking him something – perhaps why the trip was taking so long. Maybe they had flown to Nairobi before and knew that they should have been there by now. The trip should only have taken one and a half hours, but we had now been flying for over three.

However, after another event-free hour, the tedium of the situation had strangely dissipated our panic. We had actually got used to the idea that we were in a hijacked plane; that we had no idea where we were going or what was going to happen to us next. But then, just as we began to feel more secure, some of the other passengers became fidgety. The Israeli businessmen had actually got up out of their seats and were standing chatting to one another. I felt intensely irritated by this apparent show of indifference to our situation. No-one had given us permission to move around and I didn't want anyone to give the hijackers an excuse to leave the front of the plane.

'I just wish they would bloody well sit down,' I muttered to Lizzie.

'I know.' She was obviously equally annoyed. 'This is hardly the time to have a gossip with your mates.'

We watched in disbelief as they chatted and laughed. It crossed our minds that maybe they were more used to terrorism in Israel. Their country, we reminded ourselves, was constantly under threat of war. But they seemed so calm and comfortable it was as if this was just another daily occurrence. They certainly didn't look like people who believed they were about to be blown up. Perhaps they were trying to instil confidence in the rest of us, or perhaps they had a better idea of what was really going on. Maybe they were just chatting among themselves in the same way that we had, as a distraction from the fear. But the truth was, we didn't have a clue. We had no idea what was going on or who anybody was, including the hijackers. We had no way of knowing if the man sitting behind us was part of the team. We didn't know where we were going or how long it was going to last. We didn't know who to trust or who to fear.

This one small incident scratched our surface calm and allowed all the terrors to escape again. We could feel our anxiety levels rising and realised that we were still walking a tightrope. If the rope shook too violently we would be plunging headlong into emotions we wouldn't be able to control.

The ropes were given a further wobble as a man moved back from four or five rows further up the plane and took the seat in front of us. It was impossible to tell what nationality he was or why he felt confident enough to select his own seat at such a tense time. Was he one of them? Or was he someone who was going to challenge them and cause them to lose control? We both felt deeply afraid of him.

After smoking a cigarette he stood up, causing both our hearts to miss a beat, and walked back to his original seat. He opened an overhead locker and pulled out a bottle of J&B whisky which he started to take a generous swig from. What made him think he could drink when no-one had given him permission? What would happen if he got drunk? Would he cause a fight? My terror was rising with each gulp he took from the bottle. I longed to shout at him to stop; to tell him he must remain sober for all our sakes. The last thing we wanted was an unpredictable drunk on board. But I was too frightened to speak up, so we sat still and stared at the back of his head. He was thin, quite tall, dark haired, clean shaven and dressed so casually that he looked rather scruffy. He seemed to be travelling alone. He had probably been sitting in the non-smoking section and courteously moved in order to have a cigarette. But at this point we trusted nobody and suspected everybody.

There was more movement at the front of the cabin and we craned our necks to see who it was. A man wearing the uniform of a pilot or co-pilot was coming out of the loo, his shirt and tie in disarray. However, despite having no jacket on and looking rather bedraggled, he seemed surprisingly relaxed. He smiled down the plane and made the same movement with his hands as the stewardess had done, indicating that all was well. He chatted to the Israeli businessmen and his composure raised our spirits a little. He looked like a man who knew what he was doing and he didn't seem to be registering any sort of panic. He walked back up the plane and disappeared. Everything was going to be OK and we were sure now that our ordeal would be over quite soon.

*

Both Lizzie and I were nearing the end of our books when the plane slid dramatically to the left, making our stomachs lurch. 'What on earth do you think that was?' I asked Lizzie.

'I don't know, but it won't be anything to do with the

situation. The pilot will just be doing what the hijackers want. Maybe it was a cross-wind.'

A few seconds later, the tannoy burst into life for the first time since the hijackers had made their announcement. It was the captain speaking. 'We have just run out of fuel in our right-hand engine and we are about to run out of fuel in our left-hand engine. Prepare for a crash landing, that's all I have to say. Do what you want to the hijackers.'

The captain's voice did not sound particularly panicked, just incredibly monotone. He sounded so matter of fact, he could have been telling us what the weather was like.

I calmly closed my book and placed it neatly in the seat pocket in front of me. 'Well, that's that then,' I said matter of factly to Lizzie.

At no stage in the previous four hours had it occurred to us that we were going to have to endure a crash. Once the initial fear of the bomb had passed, it had been replaced by a fear of the invisible hijackers at the front of the plane and what they might do to us. When they had not emerged or done anything to harm us, that fear too had subsided and we had been preparing ourselves for an uncomfortable ordeal on the tarmac somewhere. Our minds had dealt with all these options; even accepted them. Now this new information had arrived from nowhere and our brains were in no way prepared for it. It was my worst nightmare come true. I was going to be crashing into the Indian Ocean, into shark-infested waters. It was the one thing I feared most, the one thing which everyone had always told me was so statistically unlikely it was barely worth thinking about.

My mind simply refused to comprehend the information which had just been fed into it.

We had never expected this. My initial fear of an explosion was suddenly washed away by a new terror. Now I knew that nobody could save us. There wasn't going to be an SAS-type rescue, women and children were not going to be released and I wasn't going to be writing home with my hijacking story. We were going to crash.

I looked at Lizzie and saw her skin had turned grey and her cheek was shaking. She was deeply frightened. As I looked into her eyes I knew she was expecting to die. Neither of us spoke. We just stared at one another, too scared to vocalise our fears. Were we going to live or die? What did crashing in an aeroplane mean? I had no idea. It seemed surreal. I wanted to say, 'Excuse me, can you run that one by me again? I thought for a moment you said we were going to crash.' But the information was actually crystal clear: 'Prepare for a crash landing.' It was insane. What the hell was going on? There was nothing more to say. It was all over. I had no expectations of what would happen next or whether I would live or die.

In a perverse way, it was a comfort to know that all decisions had been taken out of our hands. There was nothing we could do to influence the train of events from now on, so we didn't have to worry about whether we were making the right decisions or doing the right things. Something or somebody bigger than us was now in charge and we just had to trust that everything would be all right. Somebody once told me that the arms of God are longer than the arms of those who want to hurt you. All I knew was our destiny was now in His hands. There was no way of escape. All we could do was try to prepare ourselves, but whether for life or death we didn't know. I simply didn't know what was coming next, apart from the fact that we were going to plunge from 37,000 feet into the sea.

I looked at Lizzie, trying to reassure her with my eyes since I couldn't find any words. Her face mirrored my own explosion of fear. We were so used to getting out of scrapes together, feeding off each other's strength and confidence. But now neither of us had any left to give. Somehow we had to strap ourselves down emotionally with whatever strength we could muster. As we stared into one another's eyes, we struggled to get across to the other side of the barrier of fear which was immobilising us.

'We are going to get through this,' I said after what seemed like an age. 'We're going to be OK.' I'm not sure I believed my own words but at least they got us moving to the next stage.

I saw my words register on her face and she started to think practically again. 'We're over the sea,' she reminded me, fiddling under her seat for her life jacket. I followed her lead and found mine. Looking around, I saw that other passengers were doing the same. I had watched cabin crews go through the safety procedures hundreds of times but had never before actually discovered the exact whereabouts of the jackets. Lizzie pulled hers out vigorously a few seconds before me and we both focused our attention on the yellow packages that were now in our hands. It was a relief to be able to do something. It stopped us from disappearing into an ether of complete panic.

Giving it my full attention, I maniacally ripped and tore at the plastic wrappings which now seemed to be a major barrier to my survival. A few moments later, the life jacket was free from its protective covering. I unravelled the deflated shape and, without pausing, pushed my head through the hole in the middle. It lay flat against my chest as I fumbled for the tapes to tie around my waist. Two white cords unrolled themselves. I stared at them, amazed at their length. They had never seemed this long in the demonstrations. I began to wrap them around my waist, working by memory to try to secure the life jacket into place.

In order to keep my emotions at bay, I concentrated on the job in hand with all the determination I could summon. Somewhere in the midst of my terror, I knew I had to keep going. I pulled the ends of the cords as tight as I could and began frantically tying knots – as many as I could – with the miles and miles of tape.

I gradually became aware of snapping noises all around me. Looking up, I saw that other people were fastening buckles on their life jackets. I looked down at the tapes and saw that I too had buckles on the end of mine. I'd done the whole thing wrong.

'I've done it wrong,' I told Lizzie. 'I'll have to undo it and start again.'

It was a hopeless situation. All that strength and energy I had focused into the one thing I thought might save my life wasn't going to work now. It felt like I had made the biggest mistake of my life and there was nobody to give me guidance. I wasn't in a classroom where a teacher would reassuringly correct my mistake. I wasn't in an office where I could cover it up. I was practically at death's door and I alone seemed to have the key which would let me out into another place where my life would be saved. I wanted desperately to scream but I knew I couldn't give up. I had to overcome this damn obstacle if I was going to live. I had to suppress my fears and keep going forward through what seemed like a minefield.

I had never before considered that shock and fear could manifest themselves in such a physical way. It became impossible to put mind over matter and stay in control of my body. It was taking on a life of its own. I struggled with the knots but realised my hands were shaking uncontrollably. Lizzie tried to help me but she was shaking too. The knots were too tight. It was impossible. We couldn't loosen them.

I was all too aware that this was taking up precious time. I had no idea how long it would be before we crashed or how long it would take us to get ready for the inevitable impact – or, indeed, what else we could do to try to save our lives.

'Leave them, then,' Lizzie said, doing up the ones which we had managed to undo. 'That'll do. It won't come off.'

We both pulled the red tabs and the life jackets inflated

noisily. The same sound came from seats all over the plane. I remember that a strange feeling of peace enveloped me as the jacket puffed up around me like a cocoon.

I had been so wrapped up in my own small world of knots and tapes that I had shut everything else out. Now I suddenly became aware of screaming. I had no idea how long it had been going on but it was terrifyingly loud. It was coming from several places but one was louder and more frightened sounding than all the others. I looked around the cabin in slow motion. My neck felt as if it was making small robotic movements which I could almost hear in my head. I was like a camera. When something caught my attention it stopped, 'ker-klunk', and stuck on the incident, my eyes staring blankly while I tried to pull the scene into focus. There would then be another 'ker-klunk' and it would move on to the next scene. I took everything in but had nowhere to store the information. I didn't know what to do with it. It was more than my brain could deal with. There was no access to memory space, no room on the emotions programmes for anything else. I was over-loaded.

I found the camera behind my eyes focusing on the three small Kenyan children. That was where the most piercing screams were coming from. They were the full, blue-lunged shrieks that only children are capable of, designed by nature to alert adults to the fact that something is terribly wrong. They provoked the desired reaction, but there was nothing we could do to help them. The sound was breaking my heart, so God alone knows how their father was feeling.

Was it only four or five hours ago that we'd played peek-a-boo with them?

It struck us that once our fleeces became wet they grew incredibly heavy. If we were about to plunge into the sea they would drag us down, so we pulled them off hurriedly. Time was surely running out now.

'We could use our fleeces to protect our heads,' Lizzie suggested, her mind working overtime to find ways of minimising the impact of whatever was to come. 'Like turbans. Just wind them round and round.'

I was about to do as she suggested when she suddenly lunged at me and ripped a potentially lethal hair grip out of my hair. She threw it to the floor.

Taken by surprise, I stared at the grip lying on the carpeting for what seemed like hours. My thoughts began to focus themselves. I realised that I felt incredibly angry, the first emotion to make its way through the mental barriers since we had been told we were going to crash. I wasn't angry about the hair grip, but about the bastards who had caused this to happen. I was suddenly furious that they were doing this to us; that we were falling from 37,000 feet into the sea with the pilot having virtually no control. What if their bomb went off on impact with the water? How were we going to survive?

We knew that we needed to be strapped in as tightly as possible. So we tightened our seatbelts to the point of cutting off the circulation in our legs. Together we went through the locations of the nearest exits. If we were going to survive this we'd have to get out as soon as we could.

Basic emergency procedure that we'd seen countless times came flooding back into our heads.

We manoeuvred ourselves into the crash position, bent forward with our heads over our knees, somewhat restricted by our inflated life jackets and the turbans around our heads which we were holding on with our arms.

We didn't talk much more after the captain had announced our impending fate. What was there to say, anyway? We knew each other so well and this wasn't the time for chit chat. It wasn't as if only one of us was going to die and the other one could take messages back to England. I could tell by Lizzie's face how she was feeling and I'm sure she could do the same. How many times had we exchanged knowing, exclusive looks in the past as a way of communicating? But they were for silly, trivial reasons. Now it was as if we both felt we needed to reserve our energies for whatever was about to happen.

Sitting there with my head in my arms, I became aware of the noise again and wondered why neither of us were screaming or even outwardly panicking. We held hands. I became aware that my head was growing very hot inside the fleece.

'I'm really thirsty,' Lizzie said. 'I can hardly swallow.'

It was hard to hear one another through the fleeces and above the screams.

Death is a very private thing. I looked at Lizzie.

'I really love you, Lizzie.'

'I really love you, too.'

The children's screams broke through into my

consciousness again and I looked across to them. Their father had put all three of them on his lap in their inflated life jackets and there was a single stream of tears running down each of his cheeks. His face looked resigned. In the face of death he was resigned to the fact that there was nothing he could do to save his children from what was about to happen to them. His pain in those moments must have been beyond anything that anyone can imagine. He had his arms around all three children, desperately trying to hold on to them all. Although completely hysterical, they sat quite still on his lap, the only movement being in their terrified, contorted faces.

There was then a strange suspension of time. It must have been fifteen minutes since the Captain's announcement. We were all ready to crash but it wasn't happening. We were still in the air; nothing had changed. It was an endless torture. I looked down the cabin and saw a lot of people standing around. Why didn't they sit down? We were crashing, for God's sake! From behind me I could hear one of the stewardesses speaking into the tannoy system, asking everyone to stay calm. These were the first instructions we had had from anyone since the captain's announcement. Her words made sense but seemed so bizarre considering our situation. How can anyone remain calm when they are plunging to their death?

A woman walked down the left-hand aisle towards the stewardesses and asked for a life jacket. It was the strangest image. She was a black woman in her early fifties. She was quite large, with greying hair, and she was wearing a skirt.

She wasn't manic or in any sort of frenzy; she was just asking for something which she believed she needed because she was going to die. My brain tried to make sense of the scene but it couldn't. Then it dawned on me that we were all going to die. We were all putting on life jackets and getting into crash positions and being asked to remain calm. Who were we kidding?

Through my thoughts I heard a voice asking the stewardess if they should assume the same positions as us. 'I don't know,' she replied. 'Do what you want.'

A young man who was sitting a couple of seats away began to shout frantically across at me. 'How do I inflate my life jacket?' He looked terrified, desperate for someone to help him. He was bordering on hysteria and needed support. Lizzie and I were lucky to have each other.

'The red one,' I shouted back. 'Pull the red one!'

'Which one, which one?' He flailed around in panic, unable to take in what I was saying and translate it into action.

'The red one,' I repeated, but to no avail. I undid my seatbelt and leant over to him. I yanked the tab and a look of huge relief spread over his face as the jacket inflated around him. He relaxed back into his seat. We stared at each other for a few minutes, then I remembered where I was, broke the gaze and re-did my seatbelt.

Lizzie was still sitting silently in the crash position and I went back into the same shape, staring down at the floor. I saw my feet in the new boots we had bought in London for our trip of a lifetime. They were just beginning to wear in and I liked them. I felt terribly sorry for them. I guessed it was too much to consider my whole self, Lizzie and our families, so I just concentrated on feeling sorry for a little part of us.

The air thickened with the smell of shit and vomit as terror took a grip on some around us and they began to lose control of their bowels and stomachs. The sounds of retching and moaning were adding to the screams. The guy who had been swigging from the bottle of J&B was paying a fearful price for his earlier actions, throwing up over and over again. The stink was almost choking us and we hugged our heads, trying to cut the whole hideous scene from our minds.

Both Lizzie and I were using every inch of our arms to protect our heads from injury. If we were going to survive this we couldn't afford to be unconscious. It was important, therefore, to try to minimise any injuries, particularly to the head.

I have a peculiar habit which is basically an elaborated version of touching wood. It involves touching my toes, heels, the floor, my nose and my forehead. I began doing this over and over again in a desperate attempt to summon up some spirits of good fortune. I've always been teased about it in the past, but when Lizzie saw what I was doing she just said, 'Will you do one for me?'

'I'm doing it for both of us,' I told her, and I saw that she now had as much faith in my superstitious ritual as I did.

Those were the last words we spoke to one another before the crash.

I became lost in my own thoughts for a few minutes. I had always imagined that if I found myself trapped in a situation like this one I would be absolutely beside myself. But there we were, just waiting, the two of us, unable to see out of a window, with no idea how soon we would hit the sea. We were sitting still, patient, and in a few minutes we would probably die, but I didn't feel like screaming. Something was keeping me under control.

I was pulled from my thoughts again by the Italian guy shaking my shoulder. 'It's OK, it's OK,' he was saying excitedly. 'We are above land.'

I looked up, staring at him blankly. I realised that I didn't know what he meant. I could no longer work out what anything meant. I didn't know what land was. I didn't know what the sea was. It was as if my brain had closed down to stop itself exploding. I was no longer able to register the screams or cries of the others. I couldn't hear anybody being sick any more. I was just disappearing into a silent, internal world. Somewhere in the distance I could hear the faint sound of one of the stewardesses crying and praying on the floor. It was as if all my senses were shutting down because I had no use for them any more. I had no need to hear, to smell, to feel, to taste or to see what was going on around me. All I needed was for my heart to keep pumping and my lungs to keep breathing. I just kept chanting inside my head, 'Please, God, don't let us die. Please, God, don't let us die.'

Then the last voices died away and the only sound left was the creaking of the plane's superstructure as it hurtled downward. I felt a slight anxiety but no more than that. I've compared it to that moment when an anaesthetic starts to work on the way to the operating theatre. My world had become half real and half dream. I was no longer aware of Lizzie or anyone else being there. I felt completely, utterly alone.

The plane wasn't nose-diving into the sea. In fact, I could have kidded myself that it was an ordinary landing apart from the occasional dramatic drops. I felt void of all emotion. Perhaps I didn't really believe I was going to die. My life seemed like the middle part of an hourglass. It had become thin, small, with hardly anything left. Our lives had been full of vitality, excitement, fun and experiences but now my brain had shut down, leaving me with the barest minimum to survive. Only one drop of sand at a time fell through to the other side.

My last thought was for Charlie. Poor Charlie. He was going to be devastated by this news. That was it.

We hit the water quite smoothly and I thought, this is going to be OK. There was still no other sound. We bounced back up and then hit the water again. This time I was thrown violently around in my seat. 'This is no worse than a really bad rollercoaster ride,' I told myself. We bounced back up again and came down on the water a third time with enormous violence. I felt something pouring over my head and wondered what it was. My sight had returned for a second and I looked forward. I saw the seat in front hurtling back towards me. Although my body was being smashed about I couldn't feel any pain. I didn't even care that it was happening any more. I didn't even particularly want it to stop. I didn't care because none of it made sense. I knew it was something I simply had to go through which would eventually end, either in death or survival. I was unaware of anything or anyone. I couldn't even register that I was on a plane any more. Things weren't happening in slow motion, but time no longer had any meaning for me. Everything in my mind had stopped working completely. The camera in my brain had run out of film. There were no more images to process so the whole thing shut down. It was 3.07 pm.

PART THREE
Afterlife

LIZZIE

A rush of water and then silence: I had no idea where I was and no clue as to whether I was alive or dead. I felt nothing: no pain, no fear, no anxiety, no emotion. It was as silent as the grave and I simply felt calm. This wasn't what I had expected. I had expected either death or sudden, frantic activity. I would know nothing more, or the plane would float and the survivors would be sent down chutes to waiting rescue boats. This was nothing like the cartoon drawings on the emergency card inserted into the seat in front of me – perky instructions telling us what to do when the plane is floating on the water. Deep down I had accepted that some of us would be killed on impact, and the rest would be bruised, bleeding and shaken – but there would be movement and noise, I was certain. There would be a struggle to undo seatbelts and a rush with Katie to the exit door behind our seats. There would be screaming and shouting; some people panicking and fighting to get out, others helping and supporting those around them. I hadn't expected everything to disappear. I hadn't expected complete silence and calm.

*

The last thing I could remember was being inside the plane thinking, I've got a 50/50 chance of getting through this. (Now, I had no idea whether I'd got through it or not.) Then water came pouring in over my head, washing away the fleeced turban. The last thing I thought about before the impact was my family, knowing that there was nothing they could do for me now. I began to think about the death of my sister, Carolyn. 'Please help me,' I asked whoever might be listening. 'This is too unfair on my family.'

If Carolyn was somewhere, listening, perhaps there was something she could do. At that moment, just before the plane hit the water, the possibility had given me some solace. I felt as if she was very close.

After a space of what must have been a few seconds, but which seemed timeless, I realised I was under the water, but my mind was working strangely. Just four-and-a-half hours ago my life had been as wide and complex as everyone else's. It had been filled with emotions and a multitude of feelings and experiences, but suddenly none of that meant anything any more. I had reached the thinnest part of the hourglass, my life and thoughts pared down to the barest minimum for survival. All the stuff of 32 years' existence and my hopes and plans for the next 40 or 50 years had vanished. There was only now.

It was as if I was in suspension and had no past and no future. My life had no meaning. Buddhists believe in living in the moment, and that seemed to be what I was doing. Everything meant nothing. I had no understanding.

Nothing made any sense. Everything was in slow motion: simple and clear. There was no emotion or fear to cloud the issues. It wasn't necessary to try to rationalise the irrational. Everything I knew was pointless. Nothing mattered. I had no thoughts of what might be coming next, although I was intrigued to find out. I was just waiting and watching to see what would happen; an observer with no control and no will to change anything.

From the beginning of the day I had been repeatedly readjusting to changing circumstances but events had gone too far for that now. My brain had given up under so much pressure. It had shut down and was functioning on a bare minimum of power, and only just functioning at that. One simple, clear realisation at a time.

I could see myself in stark detail, as if I were watching a film of my body in the water. This struck me as strange, but nothing more. I could actually watch my own body as if it had nothing to do with me. It seemed to be trapped – trying to jerk itself free of something – but I couldn't see anything holding me down or tying me up. I felt no pain or emotion. I was still calm; just observing.

Then a thought burst through. I'm going to drown! I felt surprised, not having expected to die like this but still not experiencing any panic. In a way I felt excited, as if, para-doxically, everything was going to be OK.

My body was still writhing in front of me and I knew that I needed to take a breath but I couldn't work out where I would get the air from. Since what was trapping me was invisible, there was no way out. I couldn't see the life jacket that I had been wearing, or the seat I had been sitting in, or any other parts of the plane. All I could see was my fully clothed body jerking about awkwardly in its attempts to free itself from unknown bonds, like a fish on the line. The body was reacting instinctively while the mind was detached and inquisitive.

A mild sensation of fear crept slowly in as I watched myself trying to get free without any commands from my brain. I began to pity myself, and my fears deepened. Yet I was impotent because I was outside looking in. Not once did it occur to me that if the body in front of me ceased to move, so would I. That wasn't what was happening. My mind, my soul, whatever constitutes me, seemed to be continuing on its journey whether my body took another breath or not. I felt the same as I always did, just more free. I was simply going to the next place and that was OK. I had no sense of time or place – I was just part of the cycle, and that did not make me afraid. There was no need to question it or think about it. I just had to relax and allow what would happen to happen. I was going with the flow – and there was no need to fight against it. I was just heading towards another stage in the day's journey. It really was that simple.

But as I continued to drift, all alone in my silent world, my powers of reason began to seep back. If I didn't find a way to breathe I was going to die. Yet I still had no idea how to go about it. Anticipation grew: something would happen, but I still had no expectations of what the outcome would be. Because I had no way of controlling that outcome, a sense of peace settled over me again as I continued to watch my body struggling. Once more, there was no anxiety, despite the total realisation that my life as I knew it was almost over. I felt at peace and yet almost exhilarated by the prospect of the next stage. It felt safe, and what could I do about it anyway?

My soul, I guess, was floating away, leaving my body to fend for itself. Perhaps the soul required too much energy and was being let go, as my senses had been. An instinctive release to allow my body to concentrate on surviving.

I remember clearly that everything was very bright, although I was under water. The sun must have been streaming down on the surface somewhere above and the rays still shone powerfully into the deepness. My understanding of everything was still extremely limited and this brightness confused me. I was beginning to doubt that I was still alive, but couldn't find the ability to think this through. I had lost the technique of thought, unable to anticipate the future or understand my past. So I simply concentrated on breathing and watching. The only emotion that I was aware of was mild surprise at the way things were turning out.

Slowly, in this passive state, my mind began to open up again. The sand was filtering through the narrowest funnel of the hourglass and very slowly my life and understanding were beginning to broaden out once more.

Suddenly I was within my body and my mind was once more inside looking out. My senses were awakened as if somebody had put the plug back into the socket. I was free of whatever had trapped me. I urgently needed to breathe and above me I could see the surface of the water and the brightness of the sunshine. Without doing anything myself, I was pulled towards the moving light. I burst through, back into the real world, back into the air. Choking and spluttering, I breathed the rushing air back into my lungs. I was going to be all right. I'd made it.

My life jacket had dragged me to the surface and it held me there, allowing me to bob up and down as I tried to take in what was happening, one thing at a time. Very slowly, I looked around. There was no way of knowing what would come next. It was a re-birth, and the world was new and strange.

KATIE

People say that accidents happen in slow motion and it had always seemed like that when I'd witnessed or been involved in minor ones in the past. This was different. Time had no meaning at all.

I have no memory of anything after the water came in. I don't remember undoing my seatbelt or getting out of the plane. The camera in my mind's eye had run out of film. There were no images left and even before the impact of the crash I felt that that was the end of the Katie I had known. That album was now full and I would be a new person with a different perspective on life from now on.

I have no recollection of entering the water, or of feeling it around me, but I knew I was underneath it and I was watching myself from afar. It was a vision in my mind's eye, like a reflection in a mirror. I believe that at that moment my soul left my body. I still felt the same but I wasn't living in the shell I had inhabited for the previous 31 years. I was not conscious of any thought processes but was, nevertheless, curious about my now uninhabited body. I had no images of

112

my family, and my previous life did not flash before me as the cliché goes. I had no perception of what had happened to me. I was living in the moment, not thinking about the future, because I had no hand in shaping it. I was just observing what was happening.

Now, in the confused underwater world, my body was lying horizontally, directly in front of me, spinning around while 'I myself' stayed still. The water was incredibly clear and blue and everything was dazzlingly bright around me. All my clothes seemed remarkably clean. The fleece was no longer around my head and I didn't have my life jacket on. I was aware that I was very close to death, but I don't know how I knew.

My body was facing away from me and I wondered if my eyes were open. I waited patiently while it turned to face me. Suddenly, I was staring straight into my own eyes, but it didn't feel strange at all. It was all so matter of fact – purely an answer to a question which I had asked. Yes, my eyes were open. My hair was in a normal side parting, hanging down since I was no longer wearing a hair clip.

I wasn't crying or choking or gasping for breath. I looked at my mouth. No bubbles were coming from it, or from my nose, but it didn't look as if I was holding my breath either. I was aware that there was no air left.

I'm going to drown, I thought to myself, the words loud in my head. A whisper of anxiety came and then left as quickly as it had arrived. But this is going to be OK. Peace returned and I watched my body put its head on one side as if to go to sleep.

I wasn't frightened and I wasn't trying to swim anywhere. The brightness around me increased. I felt I was going somewhere else. I had completely accepted death. I had no fear of it at all, a feeling I have since wanted to recapture. It did not seem like anything unknown, just something I was doing. I have always believed that you can't unlearn what you know, but this proved to be the exception. I now have all the same fears of death as I had before I entered the water. It has again become the great unknown, even though I've been so very close to it. Perhaps the serenity is only given to you when you're about to die in order to make the journey easier. Perhaps the living have to be afraid of death in order to fight for survival effectively.

Then, without knowing how, I had suddenly arrived at the surface, my head above water.

I have since talked about my experiences with many people, who have tried to gently rationalise what happened. 'Perhaps the brightness was the sunlight above the water,' some of them suggest. 'Perhaps you were unconscious and you saw your body in a dream.' But I don't think that's what it was. I can't describe the beauty or the taste of water to someone who has never seen or drunk it, but I know what it is like. I can't describe the feelings of relief I get when I have a drink after being desperately thirsty, but I know the feeling exists. In the same way, I know that I was on a journey to a different place and no-one will ever dissuade me of that conviction.

I have always wanted to believe in reincarnation. Now I am convinced. I wasn't dead; I just had no need for my body at that time. For some reason my soul did re-enter the same body, perhaps only seconds after it had left it, and I have to believe that means I have not yet fulfilled my purpose in this life. It was like a re-birth; a second beginning to my life. Although my fears of losing life have returned on the surface, deep down I know that death is not something to be truly feared and that when it comes we will be helped, guided and led.

On rising to the surface of the water, I had no idea what had happened. The serenity was brutally replaced by intense pain and I threw up. I saw the broken shell of the plane all around me, but couldn't work out what it meant. Hardly able to breathe, I swam to the nearest floating object – a piece of carpet. Suddenly I was back in the physical world with all its difficulties, obstacles, pain and unresolved questions. The tranquillity of the underwater experience had vanished and I was fighting for survival.

My eyes locked on to some huge gold things in the distance and I kept staring at them, trying to work out what they were. What is that? I asked myself, over and over again.

I could only see one man, who appeared to be swimming. We looked at each other briefly but didn't speak. Could either of us speak? Then I was aware of Lizzie next to me and I felt happy, despite the pain. I realised the gold things were cliffs and, then, without knowing how we got there, we were in a boat being taken to shore. My brain was desperately trying to re-boot itself and catch up with my life, but after being shut down for what must have been twenty minutes, it was going to take time to function properly again. Life was just a meaningless jumble of sensations.

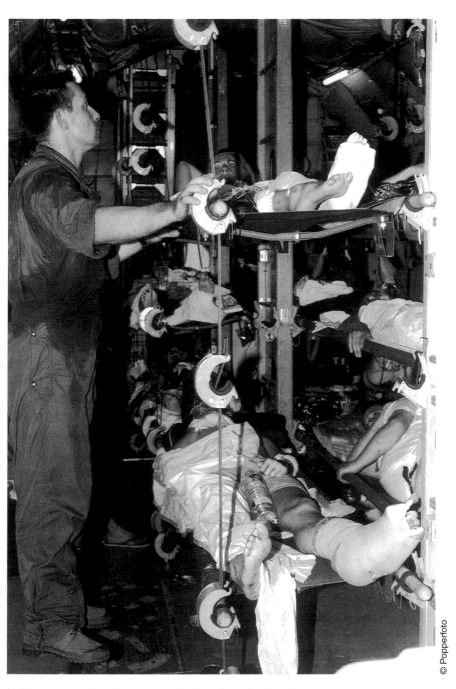

Inside the aeroplane that transported survivors to Reunion.
(Lizzie; top row. Katie; below to the right).

© Popperfoto

© Popperfoto

The final search for survivors (above and opposite).

THE SUNDAY TI

No 8,988   1 DECEMBER 1996

STYLE

CINDY CLOSE-UP

CRAWFORD'S BEAUTY SECRETS – SPECIAL INTERVIEW

THE CULTURE

THE DEMISE OF SMUT

SAUCY HUMOUR TOO TAME FOR THE SHOCKPROOF SOCIETY

MAGAZINE

Teenagers sue schools for bad ex

TWO former pupils are suing their schools for giving them a poor education in a legal test case that may unleash thousands of similar claims.

In an unprecedented move, they are basing their cases on government inspectors' reports that judged the schools to be failing their pupils. Both have been granted legal aid.

If successful, the cases would enable children at more than 200 primary and secondary schools that

were judged to be failures by inspectors to claim compensation. A further 300 schools are expected to fail by 1998 and local authorities are alarmed that huge payments will have to be met from education budgets.

The two cases follow the introduction of a new schools inspection system, which has provided pupils with evidence of teachers' failings, and a recent House of Lords

judgment that opened the way for pupils with special needs to sue authorities that fail to cater for them.

Using the ammunition provided by "failing" school reports, the two teenagers have begun legal proceedings. Both claim they failed to get the GCSEs they deserved.

One is a 17-year-old girl who left school two years ago with no GCSEs, the other a 17-year-old boy who got bad grades despite being

by Judith O'Reilly
Education Correspondent

expected to do well. Both say they got reasonable reports throughout their school careers and were expected to get respectable GCSE grades.

They are now studying in sixth-form colleges for the qualifications they missed and will have IQ tests to

back up their claims. They are suing for the costs of tuition and maintenance while they study and loss of earnings for the delay in entering the jobs market.

Lawyers believe only some pupils from "failing" schools will be able to sue, primarily those who return to education to gain the qualifications they were expected to get at school.

Jack Rabinowicz, the lawyer behind the two cases, said the gov-

errors educatic local to to imp have a is effe becaus else, h reasona the ch sequen to pick

Home and safe: hijack survivors return to Britain

On home ground: Liz Anders, left, and Katherine Hayes, survivors of the hijacked Ethiopian plane crash, flew into Heathrow to tearful reunions with families and friends yesterday. They will spend several days in hospital   *Picture: David Dyson*

Labour t for midc

Brown may start 1

A CUT in income tax for hundreds of thousands of middle-income earners will be promised by the Labour party next month when it unveils long-awaited tax proposals on which to fight the general election.

Gordon Brown, the shadow chancellor, is determined that people earning between £30,000 and £35,000 a year should no longer pay the 40p top tax rate.

The plan emerged only after last week's budget, when Labour leaders said they were surprised to find that those paying the top rate would rise from 2.1m to 2.2m next year. The level of taxable income — the amount of earnings subject to tax after allowances — on which the top rate starts will rise from £25,500 to £26,100 in April.

Although the top-rate threshold was lifted in line with inflation, more people will move into the 40% bracket because earnings are rising faster than prices.

Brown is expected to propose a sharp increase in the threshold in order to lift people out of the higher rate. Raising it to £30,000 of taxable income, for example, would cost £1.4

by Andrew Grice
Political Editor

revenue for the middle-income tax cut and a new lower rate of 10p or 15p in the pound for the low-paid, he will abolish some tax reliefs and allowances.

The shadow chancellor, who has already promised to scrap tax relief on private medical insurance for the over-60s, will finalise his "hitlist" in the next month.

He is confident of finding revenue-raising measures even though Kenneth Clarke, the chancellor, stole some of Labour's clothes by promising to raise £6.7 billion over three years by closing tax loopholes, boosting the collection rate and stamping out social security fraud.

The Tories, who last month costed Labour's spending plans at £30 billion a year, are certain to claim that Brown's tax plan will not add up. Ministers will also argue that "middle England" would be hit by the removal of other tax reliefs. They will accuse Brown of "giving with one hand and taking with the other".

Treasury figures show that

The press cover our return to the UK.

Six months later, having resumed our journey, Charlie visits us in Udaipur, Rajasthan, India.

Katie outside 'Burger King', Agra, India.

Double dating in Northern Thailand.

Hearts of Lightness, the mighty Mekong river, Laos.

Thelma and
Louise,
Yogyakarta, Java,
Indonesia.

The Great Barrier
Reef – another
day in paradise.

Lizzie waltzing
with Mathilda.

Stars in Indonesia.

LIZZIE

Gradually, as I floated in the water, my senses started to give me information. I could see an island with grey and brown rocks rising out of the sea, the land nearby covered with bright green tropical vegetation. I turned my head and saw the incongruously majestic tail of the plane, proudly bearing the green, red and gold of the Ethiopian Airlines flag, standing high in the water. The back of the passenger cabin had been torn away and bobbed in the sunlight about twenty feet away from me. The full realisation of what had just happened was dawning on me.

Turning further, I noticed cotton reels all around me. A piece of lace was draped over me like seaweed. I pulled at it to get it off without quite being able to work out what it was. The sea was warm, calm and deep blue. Where was Katie? I wanted to be with her and I began to panic. A black man swam past me and I noticed the main part of the plane floating upside down in the water about 60 feet away.

Where's Katie? Where's Katie? I kept repeating the question to myself in my head. I was surrounded by devastation and wreckage, yet it was eerily quiet. It was like a battle-field when the fighting is over and the victors have gone. Suitcases, shoes and hold-alls – the debris of death – were now appearing on the surface.

Then I saw her. I recognised the back of her T-shirt. She must have been nearly 40 feet away, but I had to let her know I was all right.

'Katie!' I screamed through my tears, but she didn't answer. Perhaps we were both dead after all. Perhaps we were in the beginnings of the afterlife, in a place similar to where we had come from so that we could come to terms with our violent deaths. Perhaps here there was no need for sound and so my shouting was pointless. But I desperately wanted to be with her. A strange buzzing sensation in my leg told me that I was injured but I had no pain, so I started to swim awkwardly towards her.

As I got closer, I could see that she was no longer wear-ing her life jacket. It must have been ripped off her, although the waist cord was still fastened round her middle. Something stranger than buoyancy had saved her, but now she was clinging to something to stay afloat and paddling at the same time. I kept screaming at her, feeling panic overwhelming me, but still she didn't answer.

I could now see that she was resting on a piece of carpet, and every so often the weight of her body would push it below the water. She would then wait patiently for it to drift back to the surface before relaxing on to it again. I grabbed a life jacket which was floating past and pulled it towards her.

'I can't breathe,' she gasped as I got to her. She was clearly in trouble and the pain I saw on her face confirmed that we were in fact alive. My initial relief at finding her was immediately clouded with fears that she might still die from whatever injuries she had sustained.

My memory began to give back selective pieces of material. My ex-boyfriend had once had a collapsed lung. 'You've probably got a collapsed lung,' I told her. 'If you just keep breathing slowly you'll get enough air to survive until help comes.'

With all my strength, I lifted her out of the water as far as I could in order to lessen the restrictions on her chest. She was clearly in enormous pain – we might be alive but our ordeal was far from over, I realised. I looked at the shore, guessing it was half a mile away. How would we get help?

I thought I could make out some small shapes moving about on the shoreline. I stared at them hard until I was able to make out that they were boats, coming towards us. I was terrified that they would be unable to see us among all the debris now on the surface. For what seemed like hours, I watched them approaching, until one of them stopped not far from us. Relief rushed through me. We'd been spotted.

'Can you swim over to us?' a voice asked.

'No,' I shouted back, knowing there was no way we could move.

Whoever was driving the boat edged it over towards us. I could see other survivors who had already been pulled on board. I saw the Swiss man who had offered us the water and the Italian who had sat across the aisle from us. Helpful hands reached down over the side and pulled Katie up by the arms as she screamed in agony. Then they pulled me in.

Katie was put on a seat on the boat, her breathing even more shallow than before. The strange buzzing in my leg was now turning to pain and I assumed it was broken or dislocated.

'Where are we?' I asked.

'Comoros,' someone said.

'Where's that?'

'Comoros.'

It was strange, not knowing where we were. After flying for four-and-a-half hours, we could have been anywhere. I was aware that I might be insulting our rescuers by not knowing where their island was, although it's curious that politeness was even an issue in such extraordinary circumstances.

They seemed surprised by our ignorance and unable to think of any way to explain it to us.

A huge wave of relief swept over me once we were out of the water. It hadn't even crossed my mind when we were fighting for our lives in the sea, but it occurred to me now that we were both prone to panic when swimming in deep water. The boat's owners then spotted another woman in the water and pulled her out. She was badly injured. Katie and I were asked to move further down so that they could lie her across the bow and start pumping her chest.

The boat had a glass bottom and the sea below was clear,

but blood was mixing with water in the bottom and sloshed from one end to the other in a series of brown waves as the craft headed for the shore with its gruesome cargo. Katie was growing paler every moment. The Swiss and Italian men told us they had been picked up hundreds of feet away from us.

As we drew closer to the shore, people waded out from the beach to meet the boat. I vividly remember what looked like a young, white honeymoon couple, holding their faces in horror and crying. It seemed odd that they should be so upset – we still had no idea of the magnitude of our situation. Our senses and minds were still working in a very limited capacity. Nothing seemed to add up. We felt vulnerable and unable to cope with anything, wholly dependent on strangers for whatever happened to us next.

We were carried off the boat one by one, everyone trying to be helpful but no-one knowing exactly what they should be doing for us. Katie was walked along the sand, supported by a group of locals who seemed to be taking her to a car. Because she appeared to have no visible injuries, two of them tried to straighten her up as she staggered between them, but she was in too much pain. She was still gasping for breath and complaining about being desperately thirsty. There was no way she could stand straight. One of the locals realised that there was something seriously wrong and took her whole weight but she fell to her knees on the sand, begging for water. She must have realised that the voices around her were speaking French.

'*De l'eau*,' she kept crying. '*De l'eau*.'

Picking her up, they carried her to a car which was parked among the palm trees at the end of the beach. As I watched, I suddenly realised that there were people everywhere, all trying to help. After the calm of the deathly quiet sea, there was now a terrible sense of panic, with a lot of shouting and arguing.

My leg was too painful for me to walk on so a stretcher was made out of a grass mat and I was also carried to a car, where I was laid out across the back seat. Every movement was excruciating. A young local guy who spoke English climbed in ahead of me and held me tightly. Desperately frightened now, I clung on to him. All I wanted was to feel safe. I didn't know where we were or where we were being taken. Inexplicably, I felt as if I was still in danger, even though everyone was trying to help me. The unfamiliar man kept soothing me and promising he would do everything he could.

'Although you and your friend are in different cars,' he reassured me, 'you are being taken to the same hospital.' I started crying.

The beach was filling with crowds now and people were staring into the car. Many of them were crying too, some sobbing uncontrollably. Katie had been put into the front seat of the car behind us but she had been unable to sit up so she was lying across the laps of the driver and a passenger. She looked in terrible pain. Through the seats she caught a glimpse of one of the pilots in the back seat, still immaculately dressed in his soaking uniform, his hat still placed perfectly on his head, which was bowed down to the floor.

Eventually, despite the growing throng of onlookers, the cars began to move. At that moment, a commotion of screaming and shouting broke out and people banged their fists on the cars, bringing the convoy to an abrupt halt – but we couldn't work out what was happening. As the panic and chaos raged in the crowd outside, my fears and anxiety grew. Suddenly I wondered what had happened to the hijackers. Were they among the other survivors being brought up on to the beach? Were they still a threat to us? We were on land, but I still felt we were under siege from these faceless people. The noise of the fists on the cars thundered in our heads and made us cry uncontrollably. There was no logic to our fears because we had lost all grasp on what was likely to be real.

The crowds were slowly cleared and we progressed for about twenty minutes along palm-lined, potholed roads. I gritted my teeth against the pain, comforting myself with the knowledge that we would soon be in the sanctuary of a hospital where we would be looked after and kept safe.

When the car stopped and I was lifted out, my eyes rested on a collection of the most basic tin huts. Gradually, it dawned on me that this was the hospital. Inside were primitive beds covered in filthy sheets. I was one of the first to arrive and was plonked on to a bed and left while they went back to see who else needed help. The pain forced me to lie on my back, unable to move in any direction. All I could see was ceilings or the sky and occasionally the faces of people peering over me. I couldn't believe this was what I'd pinned so much hope on.

From the corner of my eye, I saw Katie being brought in and dumped on a mattress on the floor. The room filled up with the injured, many of them pumping blood from gaping, sinewy cuts, adding to the already unhygienic surroundings. Surviving had brought its own worries and anxieties. Rather than feeling calm and secure, we were now enmeshed in a frightening struggle. Again we had been thrown into the unknown. Katie disappeared from my vision in the mayhem.

The local man who had comforted me in the car formally introduced himself as Abdalla. He was a slim, attractive nineteen-year-old, not much taller than me, who spoke only a little English, with a broken accent, but worked like an angel to try to alleviate some of the suffering all around the room. His clear features and smile seemed to ease our worries. In the face of so much horror, he somehow kept smiling and comforting people, giving strength to those who needed it. He must have been frightened half to death himself by what he was having to deal with.

He explained that he had heard about the crash and immediately made his way to the beach to offer whatever help he could. He held my hand as I cried, telling me that the doctors would soon be with me. He removed my shoes and tried to make me comfortable (an impossible task as I was still in my soaking clothes), chatting about anything that came into his head to distract me from the pain. He took my details to give to the authorities. He told me that he loved speaking English and had big dreams. He was angry with the teachers on Comoros for always going on strike when they should have been teaching him and told me that his parents were too poor to send him to university. He was obviously clever but, more importantly for me that day, he was also the kindest, most helpful, understanding, supportive and genuine person.

He knew that I had broken one leg and when he examined a wound on the other one, said he thought I might have broken that one, too. 'I can see the bone,' he told me, in a remarkably calm voice.

'I'm worried about Katie,' I kept telling him. 'I'm worried she may have died.'

'Don't worry,' he assured me. 'She still in this room, OK. If anyone leaves room it means they dead.'

Then I spotted her, sitting twisted on a mattress at the other end of the room, still breathing but obviously finding it increasingly difficult. People were suggesting that she should lie down because they assumed she was in shock.

'I can't lie down,' she gasped back at them, and they moved on to more apparently urgent cases.

I knew I couldn't move so I asked Abdalla to see how she was doing. She looked very grey and I thought she should be getting some help. It was taking all her energy just to get air into her lungs. Abdalla tried to make her more comfortable, removing her shoes and bum bag to free her of any constrictions.

The Ethiopian gynaecologist who had been next to me on the plane was now in the bed beside me. Irrationally, I found myself thinking, You're a doctor – do something! Obviously he was in no fit state to do anything but there were so many people dying and in need of help I thought everyone should be helping. I now know that he was no more able to help anyone than Katie or I, but I felt impatient and desperate for someone to appreciate the seriousness of the situation.

It must have been almost two hours before a doctor got to me. Every few minutes Abdalla would explain to us that there were a lot of very serious injuries, but assured us that someone would get to us as soon as possible. When he did arrive, Abdalla translated for me. The doctor felt my ankle, which was now agony, and said something.

'He is going to reset the bones,' Abdalla told me, gripping my hand hard, knowing that there were no painkillers available.

The doctor pulled the bones apart and then snapped them loudly back together. I screamed at the sudden, intense sharpness of the pain and clung on to Abdalla. Once the bones were back in line, the doctor was able to bind them and the pain started to subside a little.

Over the next few hours, more doctors started to arrive at the hospital from the beach. By an extraordinary coincidence, there had been a convention of French and South African doctors staying at a hotel by the water. One of them examined Katie, the first real human contact she had had since arriving at the hospital several hours earlier. He was wearing a pair of bright green shorts and had sand all down his back from where he had been lying on the beach when the plane came down into the bay before his eyes. He obviously hadn't stopped working since we came ashore. I watched as he leant over Katie and tapped her back.

'Pneumothorax – intensive care!' he shouted at a passing helper.

'I don't know what's wrong with her,' the helper protested.

'I do,' he said. 'I'm a doctor.'

Katie looked up in her pain, still breathless, confused and unclear about what he was saying. She didn't understand what the diagnosis meant any more than the helper did. She wanted to know if she was going to die but everyone was babbling in French around her. The whole scene was one that only nightmares are made of, and it was all the more horrific for the fact that we couldn't understand anyone. Katie tried to remember the words but the tenses deserted her.

'*Je suis mort?*' she cried. '*Je suis mort?*' (I am dead?)

They looked at her blankly, assuming, I suppose, that she was delirious with shock.

Whatever the doctor had decided was obviously serious because within seconds she was being carried out from the tin hut. I panicked, twisting Abdalla's words in my mind: 'Anyone who leaves this room is dead.'

'What's happening to her?' I wanted to know, desperate to get up and go with her yet knowing my legs couldn't possibly support my weight.

'OK.' Abdalla tried to soothe me. 'I will go and find out what is happening.'

He disappeared and the minutes ticked by horribly slowly as I stared at the door, waiting for his return. When he arrived, he was running. 'They are taking her to the other, bigger hospital in an ambulance.'

'I have to go with her,' I shouted. 'I insist on going with her!'

Abdalla, clearly shocked at the sight of my tears, ran off again to try to organise something and returned triumphant, having managed to organise another 'ambulance' for me.

The ambulances were no more than basic trucks with patients laid out on the bare metal floors. Both Katie and I were lifted up on stretchers and willing hands tried to suspend us above the bodies below. In both cases, the attempts failed and we were dropped on to the people beneath, who were like casualties of war being shipped off the battlefield. They screamed in panic and pain.

The helpers then clambered among the wounded, trying to repair the damage, accidentally stepping on bodies and kicking people as they wrestled with the stretchers. Eventually they managed to secure us and we made the 40-minute drive along bumpy roads, staring up at the glorious blue sky and the tops of the palm trees as we concentrated on trying to beat the pain that jarred us with every pothole. Not having blue flashing lights or sirens, the driver leant on his horn all the way, clearing any traffic that might have been on the road. Katie's breathing was not getting any better.

Abdalla had climbed in behind me and was carrying our boots and Katie's bum bag, guarding them conscientiously for us. When we reached the hospital gates, however, he wasn't allowed in and was told to climb out of the truck. I felt desperately alone and vulnerable, seeing his friendly face going.

'I will come back and see you tomorrow,' Abdalla promised, and he kept his word. He told me later that after leaving us he went home and cried. 'I could not sleep,' he said, 'because of everything that had happened.' We swapped addresses and promised to keep in touch. We still write, and all his letters start with, 'How is your healthy?'

Leaving Abdalla, I was carried inside the new hospital into a room with two beds, in an area which seemed to be for patients to be diagnosed and admitted. To my immense relief, Katie was already in the other bed, but my relief quickly turned to anxiety when I saw how much distress and pain she was in. The doctors had now realised that she had broken her ribs and punctured her lungs and were giving her serious attention.

As they examined her chest, I saw two huge, bloody cuts across her rib cage. I assumed they were going to have to operate in order to drain and re-inflate her lungs. I tried to talk to her but she was falling in and out of consciousness and the only thing I could understand was that she was in pain and was thirsty and wanted water.

She was surrounded now by people who seemed to understand what her problem was, but I couldn't bear the feeling that the nightmare was still going on. Surely we had been through enough? We had survived the crash and we had got to a hospital but still the pain and the fear and the anxiety continued. The threat of death still hung over us. We had no idea if the hijackers were in the same room, or if Katie's wounds were life threatening, or what anyone was saying around us. It was all so exhausting.

As they wheeled her out I started to cry hysterically. I wanted to know where they were taking her but I wasn't told anything. They didn't seem to understand that we were friends and needed to be together. I desperately wanted to focus on her. I have never been very good at dealing with my own problems, but dealing with someone else's predicament helps me to be more positive.

'Just hold on, Katie,' I shouted after her. 'Just a little bit longer.'

She seemed to be getting worse. I might never see her alive again. She had always been so enormously strong and full of vitality and there she was, fading away. I felt more scared, lonely and vulnerable than I have ever felt. I was helpless, unable to do anything to help my closest friend. The reality of what was happening seemed to be too much to handle alone and now I didn't even have Abdalla's cheerful chatter to distract me.

The doctors then turned their attention to me, but I was only interested in Katie. 'She's my friend,' I shouted. 'Is she going to be all right?' My French is poor and their English wasn't any better. Then someone arrived who was trying to put together a list of survivors. I attempted to explain who I was and who my friend was. I thought I was making myself clear but I couldn't be sure. I still had a wet money belt around my waist and our passports were inside. I struggled with the zip and pulled them out, flourishing them in the air and trying to explain that we were both still alive.

A man who saw my distress asked if there was anybody he should call. 'I am from the United Nations,' he explained, and I gave him our names. I asked him to call my father in England and let him know we were both alive. He took down the information. 'I will try,' he promised, and disappeared.

More strange faces came and went. I wanted to be with someone I could trust, and I couldn't trust strangers. Someone took the passports and I was wheeled out of the room on a trolley.

'You are going to X-ray,' someone told me. For some reason, the words filled me with a sense that things might be starting to return to normality. But, just as I started to relax, the smiling porters wheeled me into what looked like an antiquated photocopying room in the bowels of some long-lost company from the 1950s. In order to take the picture, the patient was expected to climb on top of the machine, putting weight on the offending bones. It was agony but I got through it. I could now bear more pain than I would have thought possible. On the way out of the room I saw one of the Israeli travellers from the airport. He too was lying on a trolley, being wheeled towards X-ray. He looked sad and exhausted but not in any pain.

'Are you OK?' I asked.

'No,' he replied, sounding resigned and hopeless. 'I can't find my friend. I don't know if he is alive or dead.' He didn't say anything else, but lay there shaking his head and repeating, 'I can't find my friend.'

I felt privileged that at least I knew that Katie was alive. I felt desperately sorry for him and could imagine his misery only too easily. The chances of any of us surviving such a terrible accident had been slight; the odds against two friends surviving together must have been phenomenal. I knew that his friend was probably dead and the frightened look in his eyes mirrored my own panic. I felt a surge of anger at the unfairness and pointlessness of it all. His friend, who had smiled so sweetly at us earlier in the day, couldn't have been more than 22.

I was pushed away down a long corridor to a room which contained more survivors. Inside were two women, one from the Philippines and one from India. Neither seemed to have serious injuries.

'We are in Comoros,' the Filipino kept telling me. 'This is not a good place to be – we're all going to Mayotte.'

I didn't know where Mayotte was.

'It is a short plane ride away,' she explained. 'There the medical facilities are far superior.' I saw that her feet had been bandaged as she chatted away. I was amazed by how blasé she was about everything. After about half an hour, her husband, an American diplomat, was wheeled into the room, surrounded by people eager to please him. He seemed like a man who would be informed. He would know things we didn't.

'What happened on the plane?' I asked, once his entourage had left him alone. Now I could begin to piece the story together. 'Who were the hijackers?'

'There were three of them apparently,' he said, but that was it.

For the next few hours I kept hearing that we were going to be moved to another island. 'Where is my friend?' I asked everyone who entered my limited line of vision, but none of them seemed to be listening. The diplomat could see that I was being ignored and eventually tried to help me by screaming at the nurses to do something. It wasn't long, however, before he returned to his own worries. His main concern seemed to be where his shoes had got to. Apparently, they had a special instep and cost $600. It seemed to me a strange thing to focus on when he and his wife had just escaped death by a whisker.

The next man to come and talk to me said he was from the FBI and wanted to ask me some questions. It was a huge relief to talk to someone who spoke English, and the fact that he was from the FBI filled me with an overwhelming sense of security. I assumed that the authorities were sorting everything out now and we would soon find out the truth about what had happened – and that made me feel a lot better.

The Indian woman had a four-year-old child with her, who like her mother didn't seem to be too hurt. I discovered later that all these people had been sitting at the front of the plane in first class. We had escaped simply because it had broken open right beside our seats and we had been expelled into the sea by the impact. People in other parts of the cabin had remained trapped inside the fuselage, their inflated life-jackets making it even more impossible for them to escape, even if they were still conscious and able to look for ways out. I can't bear to think about their last moments.

A nurse attached a drip to my arm but I didn't ask what was in it. I watched what she was doing and saw huge bubbles moving down the tubes towards my veins. I don't know much about medicine but I knew that wasn't right.

'N'est pas bon!' I cried out, pointing at the bubbles as they travelled towards me. The nurses looked at me sympathetically. Suddenly, I decided I had had enough anxiety for one day and, taking things into my own hands, pulled the drip off. The nurses looked concerned and shocked but didn't attempt to stop me or calm me down. They didn't try to reconnect me. I think my rantings and tears must have frightened them off. Perhaps they decided it was better not to add to my distress at that moment.

My main worry was still Katie. 'Where is my friend?' was all I kept saying, through my uncontrollable sobs. I needed to be near her. Now and then people would try to help by leaving the room for five minutes and then coming back in saying, 'Katie est ça va' (Katie is fine). My next request was always the same.

'Please take me to her.' At this, they would look perplexed and leave the room. I expect they thought the chances of us both surviving were minimal, just as I had thought about the young Israeli. They must have believed that Katie was dead but, rather than upset me further, told me she was OK. They meant well but only increased my distress by the second. It was all so surreal. I was having trouble comprehending things and getting a fix on what was real and what wasn't. Every time I tried to pursue a fact, I seemed to draw a blank.

The scale of the disaster must have sent the authorities on the little island into a complete spin. They now had a hospital full of people who spoke a variety of languages, most of which were not understood by the locals. A radio alert had gone out asking for anyone with any medical knowledge and a second language to come to the hospital.

Dr Frouard was one such volunteer. He was a dentist and spoke English. By the time he got to my bed I was very emotional and he spoke to me in a calm, reassuring voice.

'Is there anything I can do for you?' he asked.

'I want to find my friend,' I said.

Clearly seeing that I needed to be calmed down before he could do anything for me, he disappeared with a very determined look on his face. A few minutes later he returned.

'*Katie est ça va,*' he said.

'Take me to her!' I screamed, knowing he was trying to humour me like all the others, and he left the room again.

I don't think he would have returned if he had failed in his mission to find her alive. If she had turned out to be dead he wouldn't have known how to break the news to me.

I learnt later that he eventually came across a young woman in the makeshift intensive care unit, lying with her face to the wall to avoid looking at the dead bodies which were being wheeled out around her. Somehow he just knew that this still figure was my friend.

'Katie,' he said cautiously. 'I have good news for you. Your friend is alive.'

'I know,' she replied.

'You must write her a note,' he said, 'so that she knows you are all right.'

He helped her to sit up, supporting her as she struggled to write something which would convince me she was alive.

I'M OKAY. YOU'RE VERY BRAVE
I LOVE YOU LOTS
KATIE.

Katie had been through the same X-ray ordeal as I had, but they had not allowed her to leave the room afterwards because of some problem with the picture of her lungs. They had kept asking her the same question: 'Have you swallowed anything?'

Eventually, exasperated, she had snapped, 'Yes. Lots of water.'

'Ah.' They had all looked at her. 'Water, OK!' It suddenly seemed to make sense to them and they had taken her back to intensive care.

Dr Frouard burst through the doors to my room and triumphantly threw the note down in front of me. I was so relieved I started to cry again. At last I had a straw of reality which I could hang on to. Katie was alive. Now all I had to do was wait until I was taken to her and then I would feel safe again.

Katie, meanwhile, had her own problems, the main one

still being her insatiable thirst. She later described how she had wept into the pillow, convinced that she was going to die of dehydration. She had begged the doctors for a glass of water but they had all refused, not being sure what her internal injuries were. Eventually, a male nurse had rubbed a painkiller on her gums.

'That'll work,' he had said confidently, but about fifteen minutes later she had had to call him back and plead for water once more, telling him that the painkiller had had no effect. He had stroked her cheek and gave it an affectionate pinch before fetching her a beaker of water, which she had guzzled like a greedy child. While she drank, he had put more painkiller into her drip.

I could wait no longer. I was now desperate to see Katie and talk to her about everything that had happened to us. I was sick of being at the mercy of other people: pilots, hijackers and hospital staff. I wanted to regain some control over my own life, but I knew I couldn't walk under my own steam. If I was with Katie, at least one thing in my life would be familiar. I needed to see her smile.

Dr Frouard understood my predicament and he wheeled me, flat on my back on the trolley, through a maze of corridors to intensive care, where he put me on the bed next to Katie. She was still facing the wall so that she couldn't see the dead bodies, but in too much pain to move anyway. No-one had had time to bandage or even look at her wounds and, although she was finding it incredibly hard to breathe, she hadn't been given any oxygen. There was a saline drip connected to her arm. But I could tell from her voice that she was stronger than the last time I had seen her. I was so pleased just to be in the same room as her. I knew she was trying to turn round to talk to me.

'Stay where you are,' I told her. 'You don't need to move.'

'Is there anything I can get you?' Dr Frouard asked me.

'A drink would be great,' I said. 'A Coke. Thank you.'

I did most of the talking. I told her that my leg was broken. I explained how distressed I had been and she told me about the nightmare of desperately wanting something to drink but not being allowed anything.

'Oh,' I said. 'I've just asked for Coke.'

'Well, you can get me one too.'

When Dr Frouard returned with the Coke, I asked if he would get Katie one too and he disappeared again. As I sipped my drink, beginning to feel a great deal more content, an incredibly officious doctor suddenly appeared from nowhere and whipped it out of my hand.

'Who are you?' he demanded to know. 'What are you doing? You can't stay here.' He turned on his heel and stormed off with my drink.

'Katie,' I said, all my confidence draining away. I suddenly felt like a small child. 'Who is that man?'

'He's Dr Bruno,' she said. 'He's really nice. He's been taking care of me.'

'Well, he's just snatched my Coke and told me to leave.' I started to cry again.

'It's OK, Lizzie,' she said, trying to comfort me. 'He's in charge of intensive care.'

'He's like the bloody Gestapo,' I sniffed.

'He's all right. He's just really concerned about every-body and he doesn't know who you are.'

'All right,' I said, and forced myself to stop crying, still annoyed but wanting to keep the conversation going. She was definitely sounding more like her old self, which I figured must mean that she was going to recover. I felt a surge of confidence. I asked her again if she was all right. She told me she was in a lot of pain and still having diffi-culty breathing, but we still chatted on. I said I thought we'd have to go back to London now.

'No,' she said. 'Do you really think we'll have to go back? I'll be all right tomorrow. We won't have to go home. We're having such a fantastic time travelling. We'll just rest on Comoros for a while and then carry on.' Of course, with hindsight it was an impossibility, but she sounded absolutely determined and I think part of her really believed we could continue, simply because she wanted it so much.

'We'll have to wait and see,' I said doubtfully, but her show of returning strength made me laugh and I felt relieved.

Another bed was then wheeled in next to mine, carrying a serious-faced Ethiopian man of about 40 with an official-looking green peaked cap and folded jacket lying next to his pillow. He was wearing a white T-shirt and dark green trousers.

'Are you OK?' I asked.

'I'm doing OK,' he said, but seemed terribly sad and was

obviously in pain. 'Do you know how many people survived?'

'The last figure I heard was sixteen,' I told him. 'But that was a little while ago so it might have changed.'

'There must be more.' The news seemed to distress him terribly. 'There must be more. I am the captain of the plane. They had to pull me out of the cockpit from under the water and I am having difficulty breathing. I have water in my lungs. How are you doing?'

'I'm fine,' I said, feeling dreadfully sorry for him. 'That's my friend there.' I gestured at Katie's motionless back. 'We're both fine. Thank you for saving our lives.' He remained silent and although there was so much I wanted to say, I didn't want to cause him any further stress with more questions.

The two doctors returned. Dr Bruno told Dr Frouard that he needed the bed I was in.

'You can stay here to put on her plaster cast and sew up her wounds,' he said, 'but then she will have to go.'

Dr Frouard then proceeded to put the biggest, thickest, longest, heaviest, wettest plaster cast the world has ever seen on my broken ankle, cutting the legs off my jeans to get access. By the time he had finished, I needed a forklift truck to move. It took all the strength of both my arms and a pivotal seat with weights for me to be able to swing it in any direction for the next 24 hours. But I was enormously grateful for what he was doing and for his support. It was easy to understand why doctors were in short supply: all one had to do was look around and see the extent of the tragedy.

'OK,' he said, once the plastering was over. 'Now we'll sew up the cut on the other leg.'

My heart sank at the prospect but I bit my lip. Any medical attention was better than none but the idea of him going anywhere near the gaping wound was terrifying. He started by emptying a whole bottle of Betadine over the torn flesh to ensure it was disinfected; then, without any help from painkillers, he proceeded with his needlework, as if he was mending an old quilt. How I got through it, I'll never know.

Once I was plastered and sewn up, I had to leave intensive care, having already outstayed my welcome. 'I will come back and get Katie as soon as I've settled you,' Dr Frouard promised as he wheeled me away. 'I have friends working in other parts of the hospital who will be able to look after both of you.'

As we rolled back through the endless corridors, I stared up at the passing ceilings from my prone position, a view I was beginning to grow very tired of. He eventually found the room he wanted, a dingy, run-down little room with flaking paint and dirty linen on its two beds. I was carried to the farthest one and the doctor went back for Katie, leaving me in the care of more unfamiliar people.

'Where am I now?' I asked.

'This is the maternity section,' someone told me in broken English.

I waited, watching the ants marching up and down the walls, going about their business unaware of the human dramas being acted out all around them. Various friends of

Dr Frouard's dropped in to show support and find out if I needed anything. They brought me water and food, hot soup, a toothbrush and toothpaste so that I could get rid of the vile taste left in my mouth by whatever I had swallowed in the sea, and some dry clothes.

Everyone was staring at me with strange, sympathetic looks on their faces but none of them spoke English so it was impossible to hold any sort of conversation. They cut the rest of my jeans off me and I was able to clean some of the other superficial cuts and grazes on my hands and face. It was now ten at night, seven hours since we had crashed.

A quarter of an hour later, Katie was pushed down the corridor on a trolley. I could see her little face smiling and her eyes lit up at the sight of drink which was being delivered. Then they realised that the trolley was too big to get through the door.

Dr Frouard's friends lifted her on to a mattress, which they raised above their heads with the drip still in her arm, and squeezed her through the door. They then sat down on the bed with her and the mattress across their laps, unable to find any room to turn her.

'Lizzie? Lizzie?' Katie looked at me in total bewilderment and we both burst out laughing at the absurdity of the whole situation. It's strange – laughter was something I'd completely forgotten about, and for a few seconds everything seemed normal again.

Having gathered their strength, they then lifted her above their heads again, arms fully outstretched, passed her over to the other side and dropped her on to the bed which was now behind them.

Katie screamed as she landed hard on broken bones but the farcical nature of the scene was too much and we both collapsed into laughter again. It was the first time since boarding the plane that we had found anything remotely amusing and it felt like a release. To be able to talk together and search in the quagmire of tragedy and pain that we were in for a glimmer of anything that would lift our spirits was crucial. We needed to feel that everything was going to be OK, however bad it was at the time.

'Is everything OK?' Dr Frouard popped his head round the door.

'Please can I have a drink now?' Katie begged.

'I'll ask Dr Bruno,' he said, and ducked out of the room.

'Oh no,' Katie said, looking at me with desperate eyes. 'Now I've been rumbled.'

A few seconds later, Dr Bruno ran through the door, smoke virtually coming off his heels. 'Katie! Katie!' he shouted. 'Why you leave intensive care?'

'I didn't do it on my own,' she replied, sounding like a guilty schoolgirl.

'You must come back!'

The whole extraordinary procedure of getting her through the door and on to the bed was then reversed, with Katie pleading for a drink every step of the way. Dr Bruno had vanished again, however, and no-one else was going to risk going against his orders. I understood that he was concerned that her pain meant she had internal injuries and he couldn't risk her eating or drinking until he could diagnose what they were.

Once more we were separated, but at least now we both knew the other one was alive and probably going to be all right. A succession of kind people sat with me through the night, offering cigarettes and any support they could. Everyone kept saying, over and over again, 'You're so lucky.' But most of the time the language barrier meant that we could do little more than exchange sympathetic, caring looks and sweet smiles. I was never left alone, but that didn't lessen my fears. I tried to sleep but it was impossible, the horrors of the day running through my mind over and over again. I knew there were very few survivors and I found it increasingly hard to believe that both Katie and I were still alive.

Suddenly the terrible realisation hit me that I had lost Carolyn's letter. Deep regret overwhelmed me and was immediately replaced with bitter anger. I would never be able to read it. What right did these terrorists have to take my sister's words away from me? Sad and frightened, I lay trying to sleep among strangers.

The stillness of the night was broken twice by the arrival of new babies. The cycle of life seemed to be spinning out of control and I lay there listening to everything change.

I learnt later that Dr Frouard had taken Katie back to intensive care and all the way there she had said to him, 'I can't believe I'm alive. I just can't believe it!' He had grinned and pinched her, making her squeal.

'You see,' he had laughed. 'You are alive.'

When they reached intensive care, it was like Piccadilly Circus. A United Nations official asked Katie whom he should phone to say that she was alive.

'I don't know,' she said and, seeing the flabbergasted look on his face, explained, 'All my family have moved recently, and their numbers were in my address book on the plane.'

Next she was approached by an Ethiopian with an ugly gash down his forehead.

'Don't worry,' he tried to reassure her. 'I don't normally look like this.'

'Were you on the plane?' she asked.

'Yes.'

'Where were you sitting?'

'Right at the front.'

'Are you the captain?'

'No, the co-pilot.'

'I think you're the bravest man I've ever met,' she told him. 'You're a hero.'

'Thank you,' he said, tears filling his eyes as he leant across to hug her.

A flurry of people then arrived in the room, all dressed in uniforms.

'Where are you from?' Katie asked.

'Ethiopian Airways,' they replied.

'You were all on the plane?'

'No,' they replied, one of them holding her hand and all of them crying. 'We have just flown in on another plane, to try to help.'

'Please don't cry,' Katie said. 'It's OK. It's OK. We are all OK.'

Next the honorary British consul was brought to her bedside, who had to be introduced because he didn't speak a word of English. He had his daughter with him, who spoke only a few words. The consul stood, staring and smiling for a few seconds and then, ignoring the large sign above the bed saying 'NIL BY MOUTH', he dropped a packet of coconut cream wafers and a bottle of Evian on to her pillow and moved on to the next bed.

When the man from the UN next passed by her bed, Katie gave him her grandmother's telephone number in Bristol, the only one she had been able to remember. 'You must refer to me as Kathryn,' she warned. 'That's how she knows me. Please ask her to call my father.'

He agreed to try and then produced a passenger list for the ill-fated plane, asking Katie if she knew any of them. 'Her.' She pointed to my name. 'She's alive.'

Dr Frouard stayed to talk to her throughout the night.

'Where are the hijackers?' she suddenly asked. 'Are they in the hospital?'

'No,' he replied.

'I hope they're dead!'

'You must try not to think like that,' he said. 'You must try to be Christian.'

'I know, but they frighten me. I really want to go to sleep now.'

'Not yet,' he said. 'You are strong, like my wife. You are very strong.' He then told her all about his family and about himself, his studies in Montpelier and anything else he could think of. He showed her photos to keep her conscious and talking.

When he finally left, Katie realised that she needed the loo. She beckoned for a nurse and explained.

'OK,' the nurse said. 'Can you walk?'

'I guess so.' Supported by two nurses, she staggered towards the toilet with minuscule, shuffling steps. When they finally got there, it was occupied. The nurses banged on the door and shouted and then one of them disappeared off to get a key.

Katie started crying. 'I need the toilet,' she said, over and over.

After about twenty agonising minutes, the door opened and a sleepy man poked his head out. It was clear that the room doubled as his bedroom. Shouting at him angrily, the nurse then took Katie in. Unable to bend or move in any direction, Katie got as close as she could and relieved herself, making a large puddle on the floor, much to the nurse's surprise.

They then led her back to intensive care, leaving her stranded beside the bed, unable to move herself in any direction. She could just raise enough breath to let out a few little cries of, 'Help! Help!'

An American survivor heard the feeble sound and bellowed down the ward, 'Will you please help this woman?'

'Thank you,' Katie whispered.

'It's OK,' he reassured her. 'I've broken my pelvis but my lungs are fine. I'll be your voice.'

He then proceeded to take over from Dr Frouard, chatting to her for the rest of the night.

Several times as I lay staring upward, listening to the sounds around me, I heard planes landing somewhere nearby, bringing in people to help with the disaster. At around seven in the morning the American ambassador from Nairobi arrived in my room, smiling broadly and declaring how happy he was to see me.

'You are so lucky,' he told me. 'Is there anything at all I can do for you?' He seemed very genuinely supportive. Just as he was about to leave the room, he turned and asked if he could have his photo taken with me. I was surprised but couldn't think of any reason why not. He sat down on the bed and put his arm around me.

'I want to show this to the British ambassador in Kenya,' he confided, 'to show him I'm doing his job for him.' I smiled politely and the picture was taken. I couldn't help wondering why the British ambassador wasn't there himself.

Katie heard her next visitors long before she saw them. They sounded like an approaching army as they marched down the corridors towards her. When they arrived it was more like an invasion from *Star Wars*, surrounding her bed in a sea of red and white Darth Vader outfits. They moved, as one, from bed to bed, never dividing up and talking very fast in French as they went. They flicked through Katie's charts with well-practised precision and informed her that they were moving her to the island of Reunion – another island in the Indian Ocean, close to Mauritius and east of

Comoros – but at the time somewhere else we had never heard of. We didn't know who they were but they exuded an aura of competence and authority. Later we discovered that they were emergency staff sent from Reunion, some of them firemen and scuba divers. They were led by a doctor called Eric Christophe – a George Clooney lookalike – who worked for a French emergency service called SAMU. They had all been flown in on a specially equipped Hercules-style plane, armed with drugs, painkillers, oxygen, stretchers and other emergency equipment.

Before she knew what was happening, Katie was on oxygen, her neck had been put into a brace and she was told not to move, which seemed very much at odds with the fact that she had been allowed to walk to the toilet a few hours earlier. Another drip was added and a tube was put up her nose. These guys seemed to know exactly what they were doing, and the George Clooney clone – the most effective medicine of all – worked wonders in raising her spirits. They then marched out of intensive care in search of more patients.

I heard them coming, just as she had, and was equally impressed by the way they swept into the room and took control of the situation. There were about ten of them altogether and I had no idea who they were as they examined me but, with my basic French, I gathered they were planning to airlift survivors to either Kenya or the Ile de la Reunion. They informed me curtly that I was going to Nairobi. I panicked, not knowing whether Katie was going to be sent anywhere and if so whether it would be Nairobi or Reunion. I tried to explain that my friend and I wanted to be kept together. George Clooney, who spoke the most English of the bunch, understood my concern but had no idea who my friend might be. I was back to square one. I didn't want to go to Nairobi on my own. I was frightened again, and my distress was evident as he checked my injuries. He laughed at the ten-ton plaster and commented on the blue nail polish on my toes that were poking out from the end of the cast. His colleagues made some notes on their official-looking flip pads and then they all marched away, their footsteps slowly dwindling to silence. I was left confused and anxious.

It was then about eight in the morning and people kept coming and going, some of them speaking English and others, like the honorary British consul, speaking none. He asked me, through his daughter, if I was all right and I told him I was but I didn't know what was going on. He didn't seem to have much idea either.

By this time, George Clooney had reappeared in intensive care, busily preparing the most seriously injured survivors for the trip to Reunion. He had looked at Katie's X-rays and immediately realised that the shadows which the doctors had been taking for water in her lungs were, in fact, aviation fuel. This, he knew, was a problem since it would work as an acid, burning into the lining of the lungs. It would also stop the body being able to convert oxygen to the blood stream, making it dangerous for Katie to fly at a high altitude. He had a gadget which he put to her fingers to measure the oxygen levels and while doing so he spotted the blue nail varnish on her toes. A smile of recognition appeared on his face and from then until we left the hospital we were known as 'zee blue finger sisters'. 'Zee blue finger sisters, they must be kept together,' he said, and my destination was changed from Nairobi to Reunion. I began packing all my worldly goods into a plastic bag. It was a paltry collection: Katie's wet jeans, my wet T-shirt and the toothbrush and toothpaste I had been given.

They must have decided that the risk of flying was worth taking with Katie because she – along with me and the other survivors – was wheeled out to the waiting ambulance trucks and loaded on. The fear of flying hardly took hold, so drugged up were we. Another uncomfortable journey over potholed roads took us to an airstrip. George Clooney assured me that I would find Katie waiting there for me.

'Would you mind talking to a journalist from England?' he asked, just as we were about to set off. I was surprised, not having considered that the media would be interested in the story.

'Yeah, all right,' I agreed, and he brought over a girl who was hobbling on a bandaged foot. She climbed into the truck beside me.

'What happened to your leg?' I asked.

'I just twisted my ankle,' she told me as we headed off down the bumpy road. 'The crash has been reported in England,' she explained, 'and I wanted to get a first-hand version.'

'What paper are you from?'

'The *Daily Mail*.'

I saw no reason not to talk to her as we drove along, not realising how big the story of our survival had become in the British media.

Meanwhile, Katie had reached the runway where a big military-style plane was waiting. There were people everywhere but she couldn't see anything because they had laid her stretcher on the ground, leaving her to stare up into the clear blue sky. George Clooney suddenly loomed above her. 'Would you mind having your picture taken by a journalist from England?' he asked. 'She's a friend of Lizzie's.'

'Oh,' Katie craned her neck. 'Is Lizzie here?'

'Yes, she's in the truck behind you.'

'Lizzie!' she shouted with all the breath she could manage.

I heard her voice and desperately wanted to get to her, eventually persuading someone to take my stretcher over and put it next to hers. I was shocked by the sight of her, with the neck brace on and tubes up her nose. She was wearing nothing but a thin cotton sheet. We lay together, staring straight upward, unable to look at one another as we talked and giggled about the ridiculous scene we had somehow found ourselves starring in.

'Please don't make me laugh,' she pleaded. 'It hurts!' But neither of us could stop; we were just too pleased to be reunited.

Inside, the plane was fitted out like an ambulance, our stretchers slotting neatly into the walls, one above another.

There were eighteen survivors on board in various states. I was to the side and one level higher than Katie, with the American diplomat below me. The Swiss and Italian men were sitting around the sides of the plane.

'Hallo, everybody.' The pilot's voice came over the tannoy in a strong French accent. 'Welcome on board. I think this is a safe plane, but we will just have to wait and see.'

Katie shot George Clooney a more than anxious glance. 'Katie,' he said reassuringly, 'he is joking.' Perhaps not the best-timed joke.

I was told the journey would take about four hours. I spent a lot of the time looking down at Katie, who was breathing through an oxygen mask. She was obviously uncomfortable and at one point the doctor gave her some morphine. He then peeled an orange, carefully removing all the pith, and fed it to her. They seemed to be more worried about her than I had originally thought. They kept touching her feet and constantly checking the read-out of oxygen in her blood. She began to fade in and out of consciousness.

About halfway through the flight, she came to and announced that she needed to go to the toilet.

'That is a *big* problem,' George admitted.

'I have to go,' she insisted.

'OK.' He proceeded to cut an Evian bottle in half to create a makeshift bedpan.

'You've got to be kidding,' she said, when she saw what he was planning. 'I'll just pee on the stretcher.'

'There is someone else underneath you, I'm afraid,'

George told her, 'so I don't think that would be quite fair. I could try to get a catheter in.'

'OK,' she agreed, and he attempted to insert the tube while the rest of the military staff watched with interest. Katie began to cry and I tried to lean over to console her. I told the other staff to get on with doing something else, and I noticed the American was trying to relieve himself into another Evian bottle. He saw me looking and waved me away.

I stretched down my hand and managed to grasp Katie's as George gave up with the catheter and returned to the sawn-off bottle. There was no option so Katie let him put it under her and relaxed.

'Katie,' he said after a few moments. 'The bottle is full.'

'But I haven't finished yet!'

'I think it is better that you carry on,' he said, so she did, peeing all over his hands, feeling embarrassed and humiliated.

My neck was beginning to stiffen up, probably due to major whiplash. I couldn't raise my head any more, or even use my hands to lift it. I wanted to sit up but couldn't, and I became increasingly frustrated. The only consolation to the whole sorry scene was our very own George Clooney. Every time I caught his eye I felt better.

One particular incident sticks in my mind. The Swiss guy stood up and desperately started to make conversation, trying, no doubt, to keep our spirits up. 'Why do you suppose so many Westerners survived in comparison to Africans?' he asked, crassly. 'Do you think it's because we watch more disaster movies? Or perhaps we just take more aeroplanes and know what the crash position is, or maybe more of us know how to swim?' There wasn't a lot you could say to that.

By the time we reached Reunion it was already dark. When the back of the plane opened, we were startled by an array of blue flashing lights. Out on the tarmac, a line of real ambulances were rolling up to take us to the hospital.

'You will be the last stretcher off the plane,' George told me, 'because you are the least seriously injured. There is nothing to worry about.'

I wanted my plastic bag of possessions and kept asking for it, but everyone was too busy to find it. Seeing my distress, George played the hero once more and found it. There was no end to his talents, it seemed. I clung to it tightly as I watched Katie being taken off third and put in an ambulance with George. As they carried me out, I noticed that the moon was full.

At last the message had got through. In this hospital, the Felix Guyon Hospital at St Denis, the capital of Reunion, we were put in the same room. Even better, this was a state-of-the-art, modern medical centre, a complete contrast to where we had come from: clean sheets, proper beds, everything gleaming.

Katie had already been settled in, and the room was buzzing with doctors and nurses by the time I arrived. It was such a relief to see her getting proper medical attention. Eventually, the throng started to disperse, and only one guy remained, sitting in a chair, dressed casually. Katie and I didn't take much notice of him, both of us too preoccupied with the fact that we were together again. The man stood up and introduced himself. He was about 30 years old with dark, curly hair.

'I work for *The Times* in London,' he told us. 'I'm based in South Africa and I've just flown in to see what's going on. I wonder if you would tell me what happened?' He took out his notebook and prepared to take down our whole story, which we hadn't even had time to discuss ourselves yet. We were tired, overwhelmed and still in shock. We hadn't yet grasped the extent of what had happened and certainly had no understanding of it. It was late and we wanted to be alone to talk to each other. It was the first chance we'd had to chat privately, so we asked him to leave. But he kept questioning us, unable, it seemed, to understand how we were feeling.

It felt as if we were under attack again. We hadn't spoken to our families yet, or even been washed clean of the blood and salt water which caked our skins, and yet here was a stranger, in our room, trying to make us talk. Eventually the matron of the ward asked him to leave us in peace.

'May I come back tomorrow, when you've rested?' he pleaded. The man seemed determined to get his story. The following morning he sent a note of apology and begged for an interview. Eventually we did see him but we didn't say much. We still don't know how he managed to get into the hospital that night because security was so tight that not even the honorary British consul was able to get in.

When the doctor in charge saw my plaster, he instructed someone to remove it and do a more professional job. He seemed very concerned about Katie and wanted her monitored closely.

'If the airline fuel in her lungs does not start to disperse,' he explained, 'I will need to put her on steroids.' In the meantime, she was attached to a machine that monitored the gas levels in her blood and her heartbeat. The nurses were instructed to take blood from her arteries every hour.

But despite Katie's condition, for the first time in a long while we felt safe. Katie looked across at me and said, 'Well done, chum!' Our ordeal was over, we thought, not realising that another one was about to begin. It felt as if the hourglass we had been squeezed through was finally beginning to broaden out. Stage by stage our lives were being put back together, and now we were in a hospital which reminded us that normality did in fact exist. It was like coming through into the light from a long, dark tunnel.

Then the phone next to my bed rang. I was startled, wondering how anyone could possibly know we were there. It must be for someone else, I decided, before picking it up.

'Hello,' an efficient English voice said. 'This is *Sky News*. Your parents will be in the studio in about five minutes. Are you ready to go live on the air?'

It didn't make sense to me. They wanted me to talk to my parents for the first time since the crash over the air? I told them the answer was no in the strongest possible terms, put the phone down and burst into tears.

I told Katie, who was equally horrified. Why hadn't my parents just been given the number so that they could talk to me direct?

Ten minutes later, the phone rang again and I heard my mother's voice. I was overjoyed to hear from her, and through my tears I told her about the conversation I had just had with *Sky News*.

'You're strong,' she kept saying. 'You're going to get over this.'

It was a strange, disjointed conversation and once I had hung up I felt puzzled. 'She was being very odd,' I told Katie. 'I don't know why.'

Only later did I discover what had happened. The moment news of the crash broke in the UK, *Sky News* contacted my parents. They were, it has to be said, extremely helpful in feeding as much information as they had to my parents. Desperate for news, my parents were therefore grateful and were persuaded by *Sky* to go to the studio, on the promise of a telephone link-up with me. The only catch was that they would want to record our first conversation together. My parents had decided it was a price worth paying if they got to talk to me. I will never understand why the station couldn't just give them the number so that we could talk in private first. The idea of thousands of people eavesdropping on our conversation filled me with horror. Of course I was desperate to talk to my family, but not on live television. But my parents felt indebted to *Sky* for arranging the contact at all, and must have been embarrassed when I refused to co-operate.

Everyone was put in an impossibly stressful situation. In the end my mother's voice was put out live but not mine. Something about the whole episode must have concerned *Sky* because they phoned the following day to apologise.

Katie and I still had no idea just how big the story was. Our survival had been blown up out of all proportion and our pictures were splashed everywhere, depicting us as heroes when in fact we had just been incredibly lucky. But at that time we were too preoccupied with just being alive to think about what might be happening on the other side of the world.

The worst thing for people connected to the victims of a disaster like an air crash is lack of information. The media plays a vital role in getting the story back home fast, and we appreciate that, but in their haste to get the story first, they don't always make sure they've got the facts right. The result is often misinformation, exaggeration, sensationalism and hysteria, making everything far worse for those involved. Vague, incomplete facts cause terrible concern to people desperate to know if their loved ones are alive and well. The French government had supplied us with phones so that we could talk directly to our friends and families from our beds, but from then on they rang constantly with calls from journalists and reporters. We would hang up on one person and another would ring. No-one seemed to appreciate that we were not only very sick but also emotionally vulnerable. It was much too soon to face a barrage of questions about things we still hadn't fully worked out ourselves. What was most astonishing was that no-one ever asked us how we were or showed any interest in our well-being, except one man from the *Independent* who got through to Katie. When she explained she was too tired to talk, he apologised and said that it would be better if she slept.

Eventually Katie got through to her sister and Charlie, both of whom had been put through the mill emotionally by the media's reports. At one stage they were told that I was the only British survivor, so they all believed that Katie was dead. It was hours before her parents found out that she was alive, by which time they had been through the worst pain imaginable.

At the time of the crash, Charlie had been on his way to India to meet us. He had, in fact, been changing planes at Bucharest Airport when his mother had managed to contact him with the news, not knowing at that stage if Katie was alive or dead. He had to wait 24 hours before he could get a flight back to England, during which time he had no idea if he would ever see Katie again.

Our room began to resemble a busy press office and we were in no fit state to handle it. The hospital staff tried to vet our calls and keep journalists out of the room, but they had more important things to do and we couldn't expect them to double up as as security officers and telephone operators. We were embarrassed to be adding to their already huge workloads.

Our families, we gradually discovered, were under the same sort of pressure in England. Some of the stories that were appearing, often on the front pages, were filtering through to us and all of them were inaccurate. Some said we had swum through dead bodies and sharks, while others said we had faxed home. In themselves, the errors were trivial, but they caused terrible distress to our families at a time when they were completely vulnerable. If the press were wrong about the faxes, perhaps they had got our names wrong as well, they reasoned, and we were actually dead. We were both misquoted and the sequence of events was different in every paper. One said that we undid our seatbelts before impact, which wasn't true.

My father did his best to protect us from the press, explaining to them that we did not want to give interviews. Although their home address was printed and a crowd of paparazzi soon followed, they were eventually left in peace.

Equally Katie's father found it difficult to get to work because of the film crews outside his office. A tragedy was perilously close to turning into a circus. We were celebrities by default and the other British victims were barely mentioned, in most cases not even getting a namecheck. It was insensitive that the families of these people were faced with sensationalised stories about us every day when their own relatives had died.

The questions we were asked were for the most part inane. 'Was the water cold?' was a popular one, but nobody enquired about who the hijackers might be or why they did what they did. Editors all wanted to know when we were coming home and pressurised their reporters to find out, which made our repatriation diffi-cult. There was a chance that we might have to fly home separately, an idea which made us both extremely nervous. The doctors believed that my leg needed operating on in England but didn't think Katie was ready to fly again until the oxygen had reached a better level in her blood. The pressures of the press only added to the stress and tension of being seriously ill, thousands of miles from home, after a horrific ordeal which still hadn't sunk in. We were receiving over 60 calls a day, as were our parents. The result of all this was that Katie and I had our first-ever proper argument, which considering our circumstances was hardly surprising. Interstingly, the only article that seemed truthful was by Lord Gnome in *Private Eye*, who suggested that the rest of the media had been more interested in the fact that we were photogenic than in what we had been through.

To add to an enormously stressful situation, we were being called by our travel insurance company, World Cover Direct, who were trying to organise our repatriation. We were told by the managing director that a paramedic and a nurse would be sent out to fly home with us. He would keep us posted of the details.

Dr Selik was in charge of us and, despite English being his second language, his bedside manner was impeccable. He always made sure we knew what our problems were, explaining Katie's chest X-rays to both of us and making sure we understood about all the drugs we were given. His reassuring smile gave us confidence.

We had a kind, gentle male nurse called Thierry who would tell us about Reunion as he took blood from Katie every four hours, taking her mind off the pain of the needles and building a bond of trust and friendship between us. In fact all the staff were magnificent, some of them locals and some from France or Mauritius. They bathed us soon after our arrival, cleaned up our cuts and abrasions, washed our hair and put us in matching purple and white hospital gowns.

The matron, Madame Vaultier, was a formidable and highly respected woman who we were glad to have on our side. She fended off the journalists who pounded on the doors with great protectiveness, and when we were ready to get out of bed and visit other survivors, she got hold of two long Reunion T-shirts for us.

Standing up for the first time was weird. We compared the magnificent, solid black bruises which stretched down the insides of our arms (our paramedic later told us that he had never seen bruising like it). They went from the armpit to the wrist on both arms.

We had been in bed for five days when we started walking around to see the others, Katie with her drips in tow and me on a Zimmer frame. The Italian diplomats were more mobile and had already been in to see us, so we were able to return the compliment. It was great to move, even when it was just to another room. Other survivors were beginning to discover the true extent of their injuries. Some were being sent home, while others were still unconscious or in traction with estimates of up to three more months ahead of them in the hospital. We tried hard to lift the spirits of the ward – it felt better to be doing something rather than dwelling on our own problems.

The honorary British consul in Reunion promised to be on hand to sort out anything we needed and we received a lot of comfort and support. Interflora arrived daily with bouquets of stunning flowers from family, friends and ex-work colleagues. The Prefect de la Reunion – the equivalent of the governor of the island – sent flowers and arranged for a television in our room and credit on the phones by our beds. The British honorary consul delivered toiletries, and Christian Aid and the Mormons came to visit, asking if there was anything we needed. The attention was wonderful for our morale. A British couple living on Reunion phoned and asked if they could visit, bringing fruit, chocolates, clothes, magazines and books. A woman from the American embassy called in every day to check that the diplomat had everything he needed and would always pop in to see us at the same time, loaded down with goodies.

We had been on Reunion for a few days when people from Interpol arrived in our room. They had a photograph of a West African man who looked like he was in a coma and on a life-support machine.

'Is this one of the hijackers?' one of them asked.

We were puzzled since he was obviously West African and all they had to do was ask the pilot or co-pilot, who had spent four-and-a-half hours with them. We had become friendly with three Italian survivors who worked at the Italian embassy in Addis. They told us that two people had already been arrested and were in jail on Comoros. Apparently, the captain had identified them as the hijackers.

'They are being denied medical attention,' the Italians told us, 'and their families are being given no information about them. But we know they are innocent. We were sitting near them on the plane. We call the police constantly, trying to get them released.'

Their efforts paid off and the men were set free six days later, but there was never any explanation given as to why it had happened. How could the pilot have misidentified two people when he had spent so long with them? It made no sense and still doesn't.

The support we were offered from all over the world was breathtaking. The French had sent in George Clooney and his paramedics and were paying for all our medical expenses on Reunion – a lucky break for the insurance company. Someone from the American embassy visited us every day along with the British honorary consul.

One day we received a call from the British ambassador in Madagascar. 'Are you all right?' he asked.

'Yes,' we said, not knowing what else to say.

'Is there anything you need?'

'No.' That was the last we heard. We couldn't help feeling let down by our country.

Get well wishes were pouring in from friends by the millions and eventually the hospital fax machine ground to a halt. The staff took it in good spirit and gave us another number. It was beginning to feel like being in a hotel. We were given identical gowns, bed baths and hair washes. After camping in Ethiopia, this was luxury. As the days passed and our strength grew, so did our euphoria at being alive. We giggled a lot and continuously congratulated each other on our miraculous survival.

Being involved in the crash brought bonds with unlikely people, but we were the only ones who could appreciate the enormity of what had happened and so it was natural that we should seek solace in each other. The American with the broken pelvis was still in a lot of pain. Although he was going to be there for a long time, he offered any assistance we might need. There was an Indian woman in the room next door who was still pretty much unconscious. Her brother had flown in to be with her and we filled him in on whatever information we had by then. He offered us his house if we ever made it to India. The Italians left before us and we all swapped addresses. One of them told us that he had been in a helicopter crash before where he had been the only survivor.

The ward sister marvelled at how we were keeping everyone's spirits up – but it was easy for us because we had survived and hadn't lost friends or loved ones. It felt good to be able to help.

Another call from our insurance company informed us that the paramedic and nurse were on their way. Apparently, we were now on their VIP list, presumably because our faces had been in the papers. When they arrived later that day, they moved into action immediately, checking our notes and discussing our repatriation. We had already been told that we would be leaving the next day and had let our families know. The honorary British consul informed our paramedic that he had a friend at British

Airways and had organised for us to be on the direct flight home the following day.

'I have organised the tickets,' he said. 'And all the paper-work for them to leave the country.'

However, if you are flying with injured passengers you need to have some medical code number on the booking, and it became apparent that we did not have such a number.

'Don't worry,' the paramedic told us. 'The insurance company will sort it out. We will be here to pick you up at ten tomorrow morning, to take you to the airport.'

Excited at the prospect of going home, we worked out what we would wear, took our medication, including our sleeping pills, and went to bed feeling contented.

Katie's phone woke us at eleven o'clock that night. It was the paramedic. 'There's a problem with the British Airways flight,' he told us. 'You're still flying out, but with a different airline. The flight leaves in five hours. Gather up all your medical records, right up to the most recent, and get yourselves ready.'

Katie put the phone down, got out of bed and started walking about the room in a daze, the drip trolley in tow. All the doctors had gone home by then and the hospital was virtually deserted with just a skeleton night staff.

'What on earth are you doing?' I asked wearily.

'We've got to get ready to go,' she explained. 'I've got to find our medical reports.'

I was furious. These people had been sent all the way from London to repatriate us and now Katie was being asked to do all the organising. It was almost laughable. I called the paramedic back and screamed down the phone at him. 'It is your job to do this! We are sick! You get down here now and sort it out.'

'I'll be there in twenty minutes,' he said, obviously realising he had made a mistake.

He was very apologetic when he arrived and started getting our stuff together. 'We'll be back in a couple of hours to pick you up,' he informed us. We gladly surrendered once more to the sleeping pills.

As we had predicted, the problem with the British Airways flight was, apparently, the missing code numbers, which we needed in case Katie required oxygen during the flight. Airlines don't like to worry other passengers. Even though four seats had been booked for us, a meeting was called in London to discuss whether they would take us back or not. They decided that they wouldn't.

At 3.30 in the morning, we were dragged back to consciousness and left the hospital in the dark, deeply sorry that we wouldn't be able to say goodbye to the staff who had taken such good care of us. It seemed ridiculous that we had to leave like this, in the dead of night, without letting anyone know.

An ambulance took us to the airport. Because we weren't on the British Airways direct flight, we now had to take four different planes home, including one propeller one. That meant four take-offs and four landings, plus a six-hour lay over in Johannesburg. It seemed like a sick joke and it was lucky we were drugged up to the eyeballs.

At the departure gate, we met the American diplomat and his wife. We talked about the crash again and she confessed that her first instinct on learning we were coming down into the sea was to grab food from the trolleys so that we would have rations if we had to wait to be rescued.

'When I came to the surface,' she told us, 'I thought I had landed in the trash because there was so much debris from the plane scattered around.'

'I'm taking this all the way,' her husband told us. 'If you need any help, you just call me. You know, one of the hijackers burst out of the toilet twenty minutes into the flight. Clearly that indicates gross misconduct because a plane is not allowed to take off until all its passengers are strapped in and counted. My wife tried to use the toilet twice before he came out but the door was always locked.' This was surprising news indeed.

We flew first to Mauritius where we changed for a flight to Durban, where we waited on the tarmac for a connection to Johannesburg, where we were met off the plane by another British official who wheeled us to the club lounge. There we were expected to sit on hard-backed wooden chairs, among the business men clinking their Scotches, for six hours.

Katie, astounded by this lack of compassion, began to cry through anger and frustration. 'What's wrong with you?' the British official enquired.

'I'd rather sit in a pizzeria than here,' she replied sarcastically. 'We're sick!'

'Really?' he said, surprised, and started fumbling through his book to find a pizzeria.

Katie, unable to believe he was taking her words at face value, buried her head in her hands.

'No, no,' a South African voice said. 'This is all wrong.' A man from South African Airlines motioned for us to be taken into another room where he made up two beds on sofas, brought us tea and sandwiches and made us as comfortable as he could.

'There's a hotel upstairs,' he told us. 'I don't understand why your embassy hasn't put you in a room up there.' He stayed with us for hours, providing us with the compassion and support we craved.

At one point, the paramedic and nurse wheeled us up to the Duty Free area for a short change of scene. As we passed through the terminal we came across a bunch of nuns. For some reason they walked over to Katie, picked up her Ethiopian cross, which she was still wearing around her neck, and started kissing it. We watched in astonishment as they moved off without saying anything, and decided we were too tired to go on. We went back to our room to sleep.

Eventually, it was time to board the plane for the last leg of our journey home. We were taken on before the other passengers and given first-class seats, 1A and 1B, as I needed to have my left leg on the outside and stretched forward. We were then presented with medication and in-flight duvets.

Just as we were settling down, a young British business-man walked on board and stood in front of us. 'I think there are other people waiting for those seats,' he said.

An air stewardess hurried forward to explain. 'I'm terribly sorry, sir, but these two ladies have been in an air crash. We have exactly the same seat for you on the other side of the aeroplane.'

'Don't,' he said severely, 'make your problems my problems.'

Katie and I stared at each other, unable to believe what we had just heard. We watched him as he sat down across the aisle from us and got out his reading matter for the flight – a book entitled *How To Attract New Clients*. He obviously had a lot to learn about human relations.

Before take-off, the captain introduced himself to us and reassured us that we were safe. 'You're more than welcome to fly with me any time,' he said. 'You are obviously good luck!'

Although it was a small gesture for him, it meant a great deal to us and it was nice to be around people who understood and wanted to make our journey easier. It was disappointing that British Airways hadn't felt the same. We heard that Virgin had tried to bring their direct flight from Johannesburg forward in order to take us but they hadn't been able to contact all the passengers in time. Some airlines were going out of their way to make an effort, it seemed.

The flight was turbulent but nothing compared to what we had been through and we slept like babies, waking up on touchdown at Heathrow. We had been assured that there would be no press and that we would be taken to a room to meet our families, but as the plane taxied to the gate we could see a film crew airside.

'We'll get you through,' a member of staff promised us. 'But you'll have to wait until last to come off the plane.'

We were carried down the steps to waiting wheelchairs and then pushed towards the room where our families waited.

As we turned a corner in the corridor there was an unexpected, blinding flash of cameras and television lights. We clung desperately to one another, taken by complete surprise.

'Look this way, darling!'

'One for me!'

'Just one more over here!'

It was horrible. Once again we felt as if we were under siege and, unprepared, it took an age before we had pushed through them. When we finally made it through to be reunited with our families, they had been waiting for two hours, and were lined up to greet us like at a wedding reception. It seemed so formal and everyone looked so concerned that we dissolved into fits of relieved laughter.

Charlie was clearly worried, as was my sister. We kept saying, 'It's OK, we're alive.' I can't describe what a relief it was to see so many friendly faces, but the atmosphere was tense as no-one had known what to expect. Katie asked her mum to get her a cup of tea, which she then spilled into Katie's lap in her nervousness, making us all laugh again. It finally seemed as if our ordeal was coming to an end.

The airport authority had originally set it up for the two families to be at opposite ends of the large room. Both were offered counselling services, which they declined.

Such formality was unnecessary: everybody was very high spirited. There were no emotional scenes: just smiles, hugs, kisses, happiness, jokes and laughter.

We met the managing director of World Cover Direct, our insurance company. 'Thank you for swimming,' he said to Katie. 'You would have cost me ten million if you'd drowned.' I daresay he was trying his best but the joke seemed a little out of place.

It had been one hell of a traumatic journey but now we were home. My father, being a surgeon, had organised for Katie and me to be admitted to a private hospital and the insurance company had verbally agreed to pick up the costs in the UK, even though, according to our policy, we should have gone to the NHS. This was no huge gesture on their part as the French government had paid all the costs incurred at the hospital in Reunion.

As we climbed into our ambulance, the press were hanging off the roofs trying to get just one more shot. Feeling that we would never shake them off, Katie tried a nervous joke when she spotted a red Mini with two elderly women in it.

'Oh, look, the *News of the World* are on our tail.'

My father had arranged for us to have a shared room, knowing that we didn't want to be apart. Once we were in bed, our families arrived and at last we were able to talk about our experiences in private.

Two hours later I was given a pre-med and taken down to theatre for the operation on my leg, which was 100 per cent successful. Katie was finally taken off the bleep machine and, to our delight, the hospital chef arrived to ask us what we wanted to eat. The answer was easy – cauliflower cheese, which he duly produced.

We were coming through the narrow part of the hour-glass and our lives were beginning to open out. Safely home with our families, we were able to rebuild our strength. But what preyed on our minds more than anything else was the fact that we had set off on a year-long trip and were back after a month. We felt fraudulent and slightly foolish, having said such elaborate goodbyes to everyone only a few weeks earlier. In the light of the huge trauma we'd been through, it seemed bizarre that our pride should be a concern, but we both felt the same way. We also felt bitterly cheated that our trip – what we had done of it – had faded into insignificance. We had had such a wonderful time in Ethiopia but of course people only wanted to hear about the crash. It was understandable, but we couldn't bear the fact that the trip itself – our dream trip – had been lost. The more we remembered the good times we had enjoyed in Ethiopia, the more determined we were not to allow our dream to be destroyed by strangers. We were resolved: as soon as we were strong enough we would start the trip again.

PART FOUR
The Aftermath

KATIE

Five days later, we had to leave the comfort zone of the hospital and the protective care of the staff – and rejoin the real world. We were both eager to get going, but full of trepidation at the same time. Would we be able to cope?

My parents were between houses, alternating between living with my brother and my sister, so it was decided that it would be best if we stayed with Lizzie's family initially, particularly as her father is a doctor. Our main concern was that we should be together. If the other one was out of sight, even for ten minutes, we became fearful. We were still in a state of shock and we found it easier to pretend that nothing out of the ordinary had happened, that none of what we had experienced was real, because none of it yet made any sense to us. Everyone else's reactions, however, constantly reminded us that we had been involved in something very serious indeed.

We felt euphoric in an overexcited way. We couldn't believe what we had been through or that we had survived.

We were giggly all the time and felt extraordinarily happy. A huge weight had been lifted because we were free of the terror we had suffered over the previous two weeks; we were away from alien places and back among familiar faces, and that made us unnaturally blasé about the crash itself.

Of course, everybody wanted to hear about what had happened and find out how we had coped with the nightmare itself, but it was hard to verbalise our emotions or find the words to describe the extremes that we had suffered. Having each other helped to dilute the frustration of not being able to express ourselves and avoided some of the feelings of isolation which we might otherwise have experienced. To have no-one around you who knows exactly what you have experienced must be incredibly difficult and frightening. As it was, we could comfort one another just by exchanging looks because we both understood how the other was feeling and knew what we had been through. The deep bond we had always shared had now developed into something much more complex.

We talked about our experiences to others in a pretty emotionless way, but we didn't really talk about them to one another. There didn't seem to be much need for words. Before we went to sleep, we would look at each other and smile and just say, 'Well done, chum'.

During our stay in hospital we had started to have the odd cigarette, leaning out of the window to hide the smell, but we knew that Lizzie's father, a fierce anti-smoker, would not be impressed if he came to collect us and we reeked of tobacco. We scrubbed our hands and teeth vigorously as we eagerly awaited his appearance. We had arrived at the hospital with nothing, but during the five days we had collected an extraordinary number of possessions in the way of clothes, flowers, gifts, cards, letters, chocolates, toiletries, dressing gowns and even a new pair of Oakley sunglasses each from a good friend who realised how important our original pairs had been to us.

It was an icy cold day and the ground outside was treacherously slippery, but for the first time since boarding the plane in Ethiopia, we were actually moving under our own steam, without stretchers or wheelchairs or people carrying us. Despite the dampness and greyness of the day, we were in high spirits. It would be good to be able to see our friends and families without the restrictions of visiting times.

My parents were waiting for us at Lizzie's house, along with Lizzie's mum, and the moment we walked through the door our bags were whisked away. The second we put anything down someone would rush to pick it up for us. It felt strange to walk into a parental home and not be told to 'take everything to your room' as usual. We just had to mention that we quite fancied a cup of tea, chocolate, watching a bit of television, having a glass of wine, or the ubiquitous cauliflower cheese, and whatever we had asked for would magically appear before us. We had been transformed into royalty, but we didn't feel that we had done anything to warrant such treatment. We'd just been extremely lucky – and knew how close to death we had actually been.

At first all the attention was brilliant, but inevitably we began to feel rather restricted as the days went by. We had both lived in our own homes for years and were used to having our own space. Moving back in with the family limited our independence. Naturally, everyone was very anxious to do the right thing, but this created an underlying tension and it was hard for us to indulge in any signs of depression for fear that we would worry other people. Sometimes we felt obliged to remain cheerful when we would rather have been quiet.

Charlie and all our other friends drove down from London constantly to see us and the phone was jumping with get well wishes. More flowers, cards and champagne arrived every few hours. It was a wonderful feeling to move from so much destruction and isolation to being overwhelmed with feelings of love and kindness. Others who had been on the trip in Africa sent us photos so that we would have some reminders of our weeks there. It was kind of them, but they weren't the pictures we had taken, now lost for ever. We even received signed photos from the *real* George Clooney saying, 'Next time I'll come to your aid'. We never found out who arranged that one.

Apart from having to recount 'the story' to everyone who turned up or rang, which we were still happy to do at that stage, we had nothing to do with our time but recuperate. We were fascinated to hear what everyone else had been through when they first heard the news. We needed to see those hours through other people's eyes.

I had spoken to my mum the day before boarding the

plane, so she definitely knew that we were flying from Addis Ababa that day. She was staying with my sister at the time and had just returned from a Saturday afternoon shopping trip when she turned on the five o'clock news and was told that a plane leaving Addis had crashed on Comoros. Knowing that I was flying to Nairobi, she had assumed it was a different flight but was still left with a strange feeling. There couldn't, she kept thinking, be many planes that size going out of Addis in a day.

A few seconds later, my sister, who was seven months' pregnant, walked in with her husband. 'There's been a plane crash in Africa,' Mum told them. 'A plane from Addis. I don't think it's Katie's flight but I want to watch the next news.'

My sister said that for the next hour they all busied themselves with menial chores around the house, none of them trusting themselves to speak. At six they were in front of the television again and their worst fears were confirmed as more information came through on the breaking story. They were told that the plane had been due to fly to Nairobi but had been hijacked. Now they knew for sure that it was our plane. The newsreader announced that there were some survivors and gave out emergency numbers for relatives to phone.

My brother-in-law called immediately but the lines were constantly engaged. Although the news had said there were survivors, they didn't believe that it would be us. They thought that was impossible: we were both dead, they knew, although deep down they were clinging to a shred of hope that they would be proved wrong.

More news came through. 'There was only one British survivor: Elizabeth Anderson.'

So that was it. 'They've got the name wrong,' Mum said. 'They mean Elizabeth Anders. Katie's dead!' It's impossible for them to describe to me how devastated they felt when all their worst fears of the last hour or so were suddenly confirmed. I doubt if they were able to take the news in fully as they listened, trying to understand what they were hearing without breaking down completely.

We now have very strong feelings on how disasters are reported. We appreciate that the media needs to run with the story as it breaks, but we believe it is important not to be specific about who has survived and who has died. Surely it would have been better if they had limited information to 'some survivors'. The relatives should be the first concern. Never, ever, should they be given inaccurate information.

Of course, we are thankful for the interest we received but my family should never have been put through that kind of ordeal and I find it too painful to dwell on how they got through those hours after they'd heard the initial reports. My brother-in-law kept dialling the football club where my father was, with one eye on my sister, sure that the shock was going to bring on her labour two months early.

'Bob,' he said when he at last got through to my father. 'I don't want you to panic – I already have two distraught women here – but Katie's plane has come down. There are some survivors and they have Lizzie's name wrong, but no news on Katie. There are some emergency numbers. Can I give half of them to you and you start dialling because it'll be hard to get through.' Cleverly, my brother-in-law had made sure my dad's mind was occupied and proactive.

Many of our friends had also heard the news by this point, and were all calling one another, maniacally trying to get more details. Was it true that Lizzie was alive? What state was she in? Had anyone heard if I had survived? Any of them who had contacts with organisations like Reuters rang them for more news but no-one could add anything to the story. The following few hours imprinted themselves indelibly on everyone's memories. It was like, 'Where were you when you heard JFK had been shot?'

Lizzie's mum was in the garden when the phone rang. When she picked it up, the UN official we had met in the hospital was on the line from Comoros. 'Your daughter and her friend are all right but have been in a plane crash,' he said. When the words began to make sense in her head, she imagined we had been in a light aircraft. Only later, when she was watching the news, did she realise the extent of the drama we were involved in.

Lizzie's dad tried to get hold of my parents but he only had the office number and because it was Saturday there was no reply. Eventually, after following a trail of telephone numbers, he reached my brother and told him that we were all right. The news was out – we were survivors! I told my parents about my injuries from the hospital in Reunion and we think the UN guy told Lizzie's parents about hers. *Sky* called Lizzie's parents while we were on the military aircraft out of Comoros.

We stayed with Lizzie's parents for five days before the time came to move on again. Everyone was nervous about how we would cope if we were split up, including us. It was decided that I would go with my parents to my brother's place in London. Charlie would also be with me. Lizzie was moving to her sister's London home and would be able to spend the odd night with us.

From the moment we left the hospital, the media attention increased. They continued to call us at Lizzie's parents' house wanting us to sell our story and appear on various television shows. The interest was huge, from the *Mail*, *Richard and Judy*, Sue Lawley and Breakfast TV, to *Cosmopolitan*, *Pebble Mill* and the *Express*. While we were happy to talk to people we knew, loved and trusted, we were nowhere near ready to talk to strangers about an ordeal which had changed us for ever. We didn't even feel comfortable being in the same room as people we didn't know. Anyone we didn't recognise could be one of the faceless terrorists as far as we were concerned. We wanted to be cocooned and sheltered from the world in a safe place with safe people.

In the week following the crash, Lizzie's father had collected and taped all the media coverage, but neither of us wanted to see it to start with. We didn't want to take an objective viewpoint on our very subjective experience. We were aware by now that we had made front-page news all over the country but we were nervous about reading other people's accounts of what had happened to us. Eventually we would, but at first we just weren't ready. Then, on our last night together at Lizzie's home, we plucked up the courage to go through the material together.

We were amazed by what we saw. Most stories seemed to be about a completely different plane crash. According to the journalists, Lizzie and I had 'plunged into shark-infested waters, pushed our way through dead bodies, got to the island and faxed home with news that we were OK'. The doctors had apparently said that undoing our seatbelts had saved our lives. Most surprising of all was that the other British passengers were barely mentioned. We imagined how their families must have felt, reading all about us and hearing nothing about their own loved ones. We hadn't done anything different to anyone else; we had just been lucky. Why should we suddenly be accorded celebrity status when everyone else remained nameless statistics?

We watched the television footage of the plane coming down, which had been shot by one of the tourists on the beach. It looked so different from how it had felt inside. Our memories of the incident were filled with screams and terror, none of which could be seen in the apparently calm descent of the plane towards the water. To us, it wasn't a true portrayal of what happened.

As we watched the films and read the cuttings, our euphoria at surviving and being safe began to seep away. We saw the magnitude of the horror we had been involved in through fresh eyes and knew that nobody was ever really going to understand what we had endured. And the whole thing had become so sensationalised and dramatised, yet nobody had said anything about the setting up of an official enquiry into what had happened. There had been no real investigative journalism to try to find out who the hijackers were, what they were trying to achieve and how they got on to the plane. Wallowing in the gory details seemed to be much more important than dealing with the important facts. Were we the only ones interested in the hijackers? It certainly seemed that way.

One of the hardest things we had to deal with during those days was talking to the friends and relatives of people who had died. They wanted every detail, and needed to know if their loved ones had died in pain. We tried to help but had almost no facts at all to provide them with. We felt helpless and believed that the media, the airline or the governments involved should be making some effort to shed light on to why so many people had had to die such terrible deaths. We wrote to the Italian survivors and the American businessman. We spoke to the American consul in Bombay who was a survivor and asked him if he had been able to get any more information. He hadn't but promised to pass on anything which he learnt in the future.

One journalist told us that he had a lead. 'The nine Israeli businessmen on the plane were Mossad agents,' he told us. 'I have proof that something very underhand was going on – a big cover-up.'

'Why don't you run the story?' we wanted to know, confused and frightened at the possibility of a conspiracy.

'I can't at the moment,' he confessed. 'Not without getting sued. But if the right questions were asked by you, through my paper, it would bring the whole thing to the attention of the world.'

'Then they'd sue us, wouldn't they?'

'No,' he assured us. 'You would just be innocently asking for information from a victim's point of view.'

Once again we felt terrified. We had no wish to become embroiled in any political situation with possible repercussions. These people were willing to bring down a plane full of innocent people. The thought that we might be caught up in some global conspiracy overwhelmed us. We didn't know what to do with the information, but we were sure we didn't want to give him an interview. Nevertheless, we did want answers.

Our search for information continued and we kept coming across new stories. At the moment that the plane had crashed there had been a beginners' scuba dive taking place just below the water. It was the students' first dive in the ocean. When the instructor looked up and saw an enormous shadow moving slowly across the area, his initial thought was that it was the biggest shark he had ever seen. The noise as the plane hit the surface confused him further as it was impossible to tell which direction the sound was coming from under water. He ascended to the surface and found himself amidst the wreckage. Immediately he dived down with the students to try to pull people free.

A honeymoon couple who were filming each other with their video camera saw the plane coming down. The woman thought at first it was an air display for the tourists because it was so low and close to the beach, so she kept filming. Her piece of footage became famous as it was later syndicated all round the world. Lizzie and I were sent copies of the original tape before it was edited. At first her voice is carefree and jolly, and as the plane sweeps down, we hear her saying, *'Magnifique!'*. Then her voice rapidly changes to sheer horror and all she keeps saying is, 'Shit, *horrifique!'*

More calls from journalists and relatives began to get through to us, each with more elaborate theories than the last. We heard that the Israelis were not Mossad agents but major arms dealers. We were told that the head of the Ukraine airforce and other diplomats were on the plane and that was why it was targeted. Someone said that there were two Ethiopian Airline security people on board who apparently did nothing because their training only covered the working of the X-ray machines at the airport. Despite the fact that Lizzie had met FBI agents at the crash site, the American government denied that they were there.

Just as we were starting to come to terms with the most frightening experience of our lives, our heads were being filled with more and more uncertainty. Paranoia began to set in with both of us. We needed facts, not opinions or theories, but still no concrete evidence was forthcoming. We needed, more than ever, to know who the terrorists were and why they had tried to kill us. The crash was now the only thing we could think about. At first we had thought we could put the whole episode behind us, but now the few bits of information we had went round and round in our heads. It was exhausting and boring but we

couldn't stop. Every day brought a new piece of adminis-
tration or a reason to go over events again: filling out insurance claims, replacing travel items, having counselling
sessions. Everything in our lives was crash related and yet
we never found out anything new. Knowing the story
inside out, we simply ended up burnt out. We needed to
put the subject to bed so that we could move on with our
lives.

We decided to do something positive by asking for the
truth from the British Foreign Office. I called them and
asked to be put through to the consular division. A woman
answered and I explained who I was and what I wanted to
know.

'This may sound like a stupid question,' she said. 'But
why do you want to know?'

'Well –' I took a deep breath '– somebody nearly killed
me and did succeed in killing a lot of other people, so I have
an interest in this.'

'Listen,' she said patiently, 'your plane crashed because
it ran out of fuel.'

'Yes, but it ran out of fuel because it was hijacked. Who
were the hijackers?'

'We have no interest in investigating this.' She had obviously had enough of me. 'Our job is to get you Brits home
when you get yourselves into trouble abroad!'

Shocked, I put the phone down. I couldn't believe what
she'd said. It was absurd. Her reaction moved me to write
to Malcolm Rifkind, expressing how upset we were with
the way things had been handled. He wrote back saying

how surprised he was that we were disappointed. All along the honorary consuls had gone out of their way to help us, he said. However, we were still no closer to the truth.

The Foreign Office was not willing to help, but small snippets of information continued to find their way through to us week by week, passed on by various interested parties. One call came from a friend of one of the victims.

'I was out in Addis Ababa,' he said, 'and watched a television press conference with an official from Ethiopian Airways, which they said was live. I don't know much about television but this had clearly been through an edit suite at least once. All the sound levels on the questions and answers were different.'

Later he came back to us with reports that there were three hijackers, two brothers from Ethiopia and another man from Djibouti.

'I'm told that they had no political motivation,' he said. 'The airline is saying that they know who they were and that they are all dead. Apparently, the only weapon they brought on board was something which they claimed was a bomb, although Ethiopian Airways claim it wasn't.'

'Once they were on board, the terrorists got hold of an airline axe, a fire extinguisher and a bottle of Johnny Walker whisky which they used to hit the pilot over the head. The government say they went to the hijackers' houses and found copies of the airline's in-flight magazine there – so it must have been them!'

When I thought of all the airline magazines that had

passed through my flat over the years, I realised how lucky I was not to have been locked up for terrorism!

'Ethiopian Airlines also claim that all three of them had fake passports and therefore bought legitimate tickets,' he continued, 'so it's not their fault that they got on the plane since you can't X-ray people's minds.'

We researched a little further into the technical details. Every plane carries two black boxes, one that records all the instrumentation during the flight and another that records everything that is said in or to the cockpit. We learnt that there are only two places in the world that can decode these black boxes and that the instrument recorder was sent to Farnborough in England. I called the office and one of the technicians tried to explain the procedure to me.

'Ethiopian Airways asked us to decipher the instrument black box recorder,' he explained. 'Obviously I can't say now exactly what it told us, but I can send you a copy of the report I am putting together before it becomes public knowledge.'

Hopefully, it will be ready by the summer of 1998.

'Have they sent you the voice recorder?' I asked.

'No, they won't let us have that one,' he replied. 'Neither the Comoros authorities or the airline want any help investigating the crash, which is unusual since so many people were tragically killed or involved in some way. You would think the quicker it was solved the better for everybody.'

As far as we know, nobody has heard the voice black box to this day.

Coincidentally, the Boeing investigator for the crash was

the father of somebody Lizzie knew. He was called as soon as reports of the crash were received and flew out to Comoros while we were still there to investigate why the plane broke up in the way that it did. He asked if he could see us or any of the other survivors but was denied access. He was also denied access to the plane and his enquiries were blocked by the officials on Comoros who were in charge of the investigation. He was consequently unable to prepare a report. No explanation was forthcoming, only adding to our conclusion that there was a cover-up going on.

We heard nothing from Ethiopian Airways for two months. Outrageously, no-one called us at the hospital and no-one offered us any help in getting home. Eventually, a letter arrived from their English lawyers, Beaumont and Sons. They were very sorry about the accident and asked us to put together a claim for whatever compensation we thought we were due, bearing in mind the limitations of the Warsaw Convention. They also informed us that if we challenged them in any way we wouldn't get a penny as they were not guilty of gross misconduct or gross negligence – the only ways round the convention. They said they had no legal obligation to give us any money but felt they had a moral one. Once again, if we challenged them they would retract the offer.

The Warsaw Convention was drawn up in 1929, and it was designed to stop the airline industry going bankrupt in the event of a major crash, by capping liability. It states that recompense in the USA for death of or personal injury to passengers is limited to $75,000 per person. For non-USA flight routes liability is limited to $10,000 or $20,000, depending on whether you are in the air-space of a country that has updated its agreement. Most countries are capped at $10,000. The basics of the convention are printed on the back of all airline tickets.

It's not a large amount when you consider that most of the people on the flight looked like married men with families to support. Not only have these relatives lost their loved ones, they may now be poverty stricken as well. Many of the passengers were so badly injured that they will never be able to work again, but because they are still alive they will receive significantly less. It seems astounding to us that something which was agreed in 1929 has not been updated, particularly when you consider how massively the airline industry has grown since then. Most of us have no idea that the convention even exists when we fly.

Like most travellers, we had done the right thing and taken out an insurance policy. It had cost us £400 each for a year. In the immediate aftermath of the crash, we were treated like VIPs by World Cover Direct, our insurance company. Once we had returned to London, they called to inform us that they had received our bags back from the hotel in Nairobi. They wanted to take us out to lunch to return them and talk about our claim. The paramedic who had repatriated us arrived on the agreed day with, to our surprise, the managing director of the company.

During the course of the meal – when we were told to order whatever we wanted – we asked about putting in our insurance claim. The charming, sympathetic managing director told us to put down everything, even if we weren't sure if it was correct. He said that as people don't normally survive air crashes it was an unusual and complicated claim to put together.

'Don't worry,' he said. 'If there's anything we don't think is appropriate we'll talk to you about it and amend it if necessary.'

'We didn't bother to keep receipts for anything,' I explained. 'We expected to be away for at least a year. We're keen to get going again on our trip, so we need to get a settlement to replace the things we lost.'

'I understand,' he said. 'I will personally push it through.'

Having got the business out of the way, the conversation turned to the sort of publicity that we could do together. The managing director offered to organise a press conference and introduce us to Richard Branson. We thanked him but declined – we definitely weren't ready. We could just picture all the World Cover Direct banners around the room, declaring, 'We brought them home!' He seemed disappointed that we didn't like his idea but the lunch remained amicable.

Over the next couple of weeks, we compiled a list of everything we had lost and put our claims together. We took some legal advice on the best way to do this and had the lists looked over by a lawyer before posting them off. We also enclosed a covering letter explaining that if there were any questions we would be happy to talk them through.

A month later, we had heard nothing. Every time we called, the managing director assured us that everything was fine but he just needed to make sure he could take the money from his marketing budget. He must have convinced himself that we would do some sort of promotion for the company eventually.

By now, however, we were receiving reminders from the medical specialists who had taken care of us in England, whose bills were still not paid. This was particularly embarrassing since Lizzie's father had such strong links with the hospital. Because our friends and family had been so incredibly supportive, we naively assumed that everything else would go as smoothly. It was very frustrating.

Christmas came and went and I moved in with Charlie, while Lizzie moved in with a friend. Every day we would talk and plan the continuation of our travels, still determined although a little nervous. Unlike the first time, however, we couldn't seem to muster up any enthusiasm as we approached our suggested departure date. It was all rather lethargic.

As well as the insurance claim, there were a few other things left to sort out. We needed to re-date our airline tickets, apply for new passports and replace the items we had lost. Living in an expensive city like London without an income is difficult, but as we were still chasing the settlement we couldn't do anything except wait.

Eventually we received a curt reply to our claim, offering us £250 each, unless we could provide proof of purchase for everything we'd had with us. We couldn't believe it. We'd lost absolutely everything from cameras to Walkmans, sleeping bags to rucksacks, watches to hiking boots. We were also due a payment for curtailment due to hijacking. For each 24-hour period you're supposed to get £50 but the amount is capped at £2,000. As we had now been delayed four-and-a-half months, we wanted the full amount. World Cover Direct argued that our hijacking only lasted four-and-half hours and ended when we crashed, so they offered us a derisory amount in accordance.

We were gobsmacked and furious. Where had all the friendliness and understanding gone? After more weeks of unpaid bills and difficult phone conversations, which didn't do much for our emotional states, we agreed to meet. The atmosphere was chilly. We argued our points. They argued theirs. Lizzie had claimed for a Psion organiser and the managing director made her demonstrate on his that she knew how to work it before signing the item off. They seemed to hope to invalidate our claims by proving that we were lying. As they couldn't, they eventually offered us £3,000 each. By now we were desperate to move on from this horrible situation, so although we had been advised that we were entitled to a lot more, we decided to settle.

It wasn't just the insurance money that frustrated us. It didn't seem good enough that so many people had been killed, horrifically injured or had their lives devastated, and yet nobody was taking responsibility. We still felt we were owed an explanation as to what had happened and why.

We also wanted to do something to help. A friend who works at British Airways suggested that our experience would be invaluable to them. All their flight crews are trained rigorously and regularly on emergency procedures and the next session was to focus on bombs on board and ditching into the sea.

We went to their training headquarters near Heathrow and told of our experiences on video. In our opinion, we rambled terribly and weren't much use at all, but they claimed that our testimony was very important to them. When we told them that the hijackers had apparently got hold of the airline axe, they showed us where it was kept on one of the simulators. It was right behind the cockpit door, perhaps half a metre away from the heads of the pilot and co-pilot. They were potentially giving hijackers a weapon on a plate.

They were interested in how people behaved in such an extreme situation, including the flight crew. It would be unrealistic to expect cabin crews not to panic like everyone else when facing death, and furthermore the level of noise can make it impossible for them to convey any instructions. We suggested that a tape showing the basic emergency information such as the crash position, the whereabouts of the nearest exits and how to put on life-jackets would have been more useful in the final minutes. That is, in fact, already BA policy, but as they train other airlines as well they were grateful for the reinforcement.

The most important thing for me was that the height of the tables on the backs of the seats should be changed. They are forever falling down during flights and in a full-impact situation they could cause serious injuries. In the case of small children, they are exactly at throat height and could garrotte them. We also pointed out that because the seats are so close together, anyone over six foot would have real difficulty getting into the crash position. Whether airlines would be willing to lose that extra revenue for the sake of safety, however, is another matter.

We also discovered that the reason why military aircraft seating is either along the sides or facing backward is because it increases the chances of survival in a crash. For aesthetic reasons, commercial airlines have their passengers facing forward. It is something else the airlines should seriously consider changing.

British Airways were the first strangers that we had talked through our ordeal with. We were both very nervous beforehand but the feedback we received, and the knowledge that we were doing something positive, really helped. Afterwards, they showed us around the simulators. It was the first time either of us had been near an aeroplane since arriving back in England, and it was hard to actually step inside. We grew very quiet, but the training staff led us gently by the hand, allowing us to practise opening the doors and running us through some of their procedures to help us regain our confidence.

We were both agreed that if we didn't continue our trip and allowed the hijackers to frighten us off travelling, then they would have gained even more power over our lives. Many of our friends thought we were crazy to want to jump straight back on the horse after falling off so badly, but we knew it was something we had to do. Our year-long trip had only lasted a month and we were determined not to give up.

If we were going to travel again we knew that meant flying. It didn't seem wise to just rush out blindly and start the trip in case one or both of us discovered that when it came to the crunch we couldn't get on the plane, so we decided to do a trial run to my parents' house in Greece. We figured that if we could survive this three-hour flight we would be able to restart the big trip.

The airport was heaving with people. I looked at Lizzie, sensing her nerves at the sight of the faceless crowds milling around us.

'I'm not sure I can do this,' she said.

'Don't worry,' I replied. 'We can turn back at any point. We don't have to go.'

She wasn't pale; just anxious-looking and slightly wide eyed. I wasn't panicking because we weren't on the plane yet and I knew we could back out if we needed to. I was forcing myself to suppress any fears. Gritting our teeth, we slowly made our way to the gate and checked in, still telling ourselves we could abort the mission at any stage. The man glanced at our brand-new passports.

'Nice photos,' he said, making us laugh.

He was relaxed and his calmness infected us.

We had decided not to tell the cabin crew of our predicament, but as we made our way to the back of the plane a lot of our fears started to bubble up through the thin veneer of self-control and we decided we had better tell the flight attendant.

'You shouldn't be nervous,' she said blithely when we explained our situation. 'You're lucky you survived.'

Telling her had been a mistake and we regretted it, especially when she sat down with us just prior to take-off and asked us to tell her the whole story. We told her we didn't want to talk about it, and she dropped the subject, looking a little embarrassed.

The flight was, in fact, much easier than we had anticipated, but we knew that landing was going to be the moment of truth.

When the captain came across the tannoy to tell us that there were strong winds over Athens and that we should be prepared for a bumpy landing, anxiety rose wildly inside us. We held hands tightly, supporting each other as the aircraft lurched its way down. Twenty minutes later we were on the runway, all tensions drained away, and we felt very proud of our achievement. Now we were certain that we would be able to continue our trip. It hadn't, after all, been the plane's fault we had crashed. And what were the chances of us being hijacked again? We later heard that the pilot of the Ethiopian Airways flight was voted Pilot of the Year by the International Aviation Industry. But we also heard that it was his third hijacking.

Our return flight also went without a hitch and we realised just how important it is that the captain tells passengers when he is about to start the descent and explains the changes in engine noise before they happen.

That way, your imagination isn't given a chance to start working overtime.

Although physically we had recovered remarkably well, Lizzie walking without crutches within a month and my ribs healing by January and my lungs passing all the tests, the highs and lows we experienced each day showed that our emotions were taking longer to mend.

At her final check-up, Lizzie thanked her surgeon for everything he had done. 'Don't thank me,' he said. 'You're the one who healed it.'

Nevertheless, we thought we should be proactive in seeking some counselling for the shock we had suffered. We asked World Cover Direct if we were covered for this. Unsurprisingly, we weren't.

We made separate appointments with a psychiatrist but were dismayed when we found him inhabiting a cold, plastic, sterile room, not the best environment in which to relax if you're feeling vulnerable.

'Have you ever thought you were gay?' was one of his clichéd questions to Lizzie.

'How is your libido?' he asked me.

We came to the conclusion that he wasn't going to be a great deal of help and decided that we weren't in that bad a mental shape. However, Charlie told me that I often woke up in the middle of the night, screaming at the wall, but I could never remember it in the morning. Perhaps I should get some post-traumatic stress counselling, he suggested. I agreed to give it a go.

Via a friend of Charlie's, I found a woman I felt comfortable with and started seeing her twice a week at her home. In contrast with the psychiatrist, she made me tea and ensured that I was totally relaxed before starting the sessions. She explained that it was important to get shock out of your body in the same way as you bleed when you cut yourself or bruise after a nasty bump. She didn't ask me inane questions about my sex life but made me go over the crash again and again, like repeating a film. She showed me that I was feeling a lot of things I hadn't been aware of, like being frightened of people I didn't know or of being in a packed bar or room. I think this goes back to the fact that we never found out what the hijackers looked like. I found it very difficult to identify what I was feeling. She asked where in my body I felt things and what shape or colour they were. I eventually identified the feeling as a black puff behind my eyes, which I now know symbolised death.

She talked of the grieving I would have to do for those who had died and for the person I had previously been. Then I would be able to move forward. I had to let go of who I was before and discover who I was now. She made me see that, through becoming aware of my mortality, I had become preoccupied with fears of growing old and approaching death.

I started to feel better and stronger because I had begun to accept the situation. The nightmares stopped. Remembering what happened on the plane began to make me less anxious, and I started to have time off from thinking about it. Slowly, I found fewer hours in the day were being taken up with thoughts of the crash. I began to feel calmer and less tortured.

We had talked about our out-of-body experiences but we didn't understand them, which made it difficult to explain them to others who might not believe us. Gradually, however, that became irrelevant. We knew what had happened to us and what we believed and it no longer seemed important if other people didn't understand. We became more confident with our experience and gained strength from that. We discovered what was important for our recovery and what wasn't. Being honest and not suppressing anything was the key. We realised that we, and our experiences, were more important than the fear of somebody not believing us.

I suggested that Lizzie should go through the same process. My counsellor gave us the name of a colleague for her and the same method was used. It was uplifting to be able to talk so openly to somebody unrelated emotionally and physically to the crash and still feel safe.

Although Lizzie and I had been through the same event, we were different people so there were limits to how much help and support we could be to one another. It wasn't difficult to talk about what had happened but we only had a limited understanding of events and how they had affected us. We were learning a new vocabulary and we weren't yet familiar with the words or the feelings we were experiencing. Talking to other, unconnected people helped to fill this gap. Without their help we were going round in circles, unable to advise one another or find a path out of the maze.

Neither of us had been able to get in touch with our anger, perhaps because we didn't know who to blame and so couldn't direct it. Fate gave us a new target.

We had both been living in the same area of London for fifteen years and were very familiar with the streets. One night, after a fantastic day at a friend's wedding, we went to a local restaurant for dinner. Coming out at about midnight, we looked around for a cab. We didn't see the man approaching from behind, even though the street was well lit, until he was upon us. He knocked us both to the floor and we immediately saw that he had a knife. We screamed for help but nobody came, so we just kept struggling with all our strength, overwhelmed by fear and anger. Eventually he gave up and sauntered off, leaving us sobbing with shock. Somebody must have called the police because they arrived a few seconds later. I saw the knife lying on the ground and realised just how much danger we had been in. The adrenaline was still pumping through our veins as we climbed into the back of the police car – bringing with it a sickening reminder of how we had felt during the crash – and they drove us around to see if we could find the culprit.

This time we had seen our attacker's face. We described him to the police and it became clear that he was a well-known character to them. We couldn't see him that night but we agreed to do an identity parade and anything else necessary to put him away. The police seemed concerned that we might not have the courage to testify in a crown court. We, however, were now so in touch with our anger that all the emotions we had been repressing about the hijackers bubbled to the surface and focused on this one man. We knew we would have the courage.

The police organised an identity parade but the man failed to show up. They advised us that he would probably do this a number of times and, since we were planning to fly to India in about three weeks, we reached the decision that we would have to let him get away with it. If we had postponed our departure he, like the hijackers, would have succeeded in gaining control over us. At least he had done us the service of allowing us to release our anger.

Before setting off once more, we tried to tie up as many loose ends as possible. We had instructed a lawyer to deal with Ethiopian Airways and we had been receiving calls from the lawyers of other survivors. We were all beginning to pull together at last but it was obvious that it was going to be a long time before any significant information appeared. The official report of the crash wasn't due to come out until the summer of 1998 and we knew that we had two years to make a claim against the airline.

World Cover Direct had sent us the agreed sum and had, as an afterthought, contributed towards the counselling bills. Our days leading up to our departure settled into a pattern. We would spend our mornings watching *Richard and Judy*, *Kilroy* and *Can't Cook, Won't Cook*, eating slices of toast and peanut butter, drinking tea and phoning one another to discuss what we were watching. Neither of us had seen much daytime television before and couldn't believe how wonderful it was. Having been so emotionally stretched and preoccupied for so long, light entertainment was the perfect escape. We would dare one another to call in on one of the phone lines but we never had the guts.

Lizzie would be round at my place by lunchtime and we would watch *Neighbours* together before going shopping for our travel supplies. Doing it all for a second time lacked the lustre of our first experience. We didn't have any leaving parties this time – just family dinners. Charlie was planning to meet us six weeks later in India.

We finally arranged to set out for Madras on 21 April 1997, full of trepidation and only too aware of just how badly things can go wrong. Now, when people asked us how long we would be away for, we would reply, 'Who knows? Just as long as it's our choice to return this time.' Although our tickets were booked to go right round the globe, neither of us could think ahead for much more than a month at a time. We had no idea how we were going to feel and knew now that we couldn't plan exactly what we would do when we got there.

The night before we left, we each stayed with our parents, planning to meet at Heathrow in the morning. I woke early. The television was on downstairs and I heard my father say, 'Oh, God. Jill, come and watch the news.'

I decided to get up and see what had caught his attention. My mother greeted me with a cup of tea and a Marmite muffin. I turned to look at the screen and saw that most of the London train stations were closed, as were Gatwick and Stanstead airports and most of Heathrow. The IRA had blitzed London with bomb threats. A wave of anxiety swept through me. I called Lizzie, who was still in bed and unaware of the situation. We decided not to let them beat us. We would meet as arranged and see what happened.

In fact, our terminal was relatively unaffected and we were able to check in without problems. Neither of us felt relaxed or happy, but consoled ourselves with the fact that at least security checks would be rigorous today. For the second time in six months, we waved goodbye to our families.

We were delayed about two hours before boarding. We were flying with British Airways and the crew, who knew our history, upgraded us. The pilot, the co-pilot and the chief steward all introduced themselves to us. After a wait of half an hour, the plane taxied out of the gate. Then it taxied back in again and the pilot informed us that he couldn't start engine number two.

This, we decided, was a clear sign that we should get off, but the flight crew gathered around us, assuring us that a 747 could function on three engines anyway so there wasn't a problem, although obviously they wanted everything to be working properly before setting off. The co-pilot sat with us throughout the delay, ensuring that we stayed calm.

'It's the starter motor,' he kept explaining. 'It doesn't affect the engine.'

When we did finally take off, the chief steward brought us a bottle of champagne each. Twenty minutes into the flight, the captain was on the tannoy, asking if there was a doctor on board. Of course, Lizzie and I immediately assumed that the entire crew was coming down with food poisoning and we would have to fly the plane. It turned out that another passenger was even more nervous than us and was hyperventilating.

From then on the flight was amazing and we were treated like royalty. Nine hours later we touched down in Madras and our world travels finally restarted, five months behind schedule.

We continue to believe that flying is one of the safest forms of travel but we still want to know what happened on that day in Ethiopia. There must have been a reason why a bunch of people decided to hijack a plane and cause it to crash, killing 127 people, possibly including themselves, and severely injuring and traumatising the rest. There had to be a reason and to be told 'They were just drunk' or 'They wanted to go to Australia' isn't good enough. If that's the case, it means they were able to get control of a plane without knowing what they were doing, which is somehow even worse.

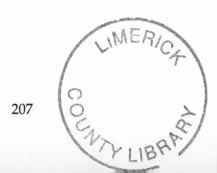

EPILOGUE

Sixteen months after the crash (having travelled though India, then travelled to Thailand, Laos, Vietnam, Hong Kong, back to Thailand, Malaysia, Indonesia and Australia)

In a funny sort of way, we've enjoyed the trip more because of what happened. We've certainly appreciated everything more, because the crash has heightened our awareness of the value of life. The colours of India and the foods of Thailand, the unspoilt jungles of Laos, the history of Vietnam, the changes in Hong Kong, the culture of Malaysia, the volcanic beauty of Indonesia and the vastness and diversity of Australia have carried us along on a magnificent learning curve. The months have been crammed with energising experiences, filling us with positivity. We've met incredible people, discovered the underwater world of scuba diving, sailed an 80-foot racing yacht, seen erupting volcanoes, been taught the spiritual way by an Indian guru, been blessed by His Holiness the Dalai Lama, trekked through the jungles of Thailand and tried and failed to get a taxi in Kuala Lumpur. We've lived in the bush in Australia and learnt to appreciate its wildlife, even when it involves sharing a toilet with a two-metre snake. We've swum in the ocean on horseback and ridden through the desert in Ladakh on the Tibetan plateau. We've been four-wheel driving across the world's largest sand island and we've drunk deeply from the many cultures of the countries we've visited. We've never felt so inspired, and we have now extended our trip to include New Zealand, Canada, the USA and Central and South America.

Since the crash there has not been a day when we haven't both sported blue toenails, just in case we should ever get separated. It's funny how, when travelling, the goal becomes having the fewest possessions possible, but neither of us is ever without the mandatory bottle of blue nail varnish tucked safely into our day packs. It is as valuable as our passports, driving licences and credit cards. We still carry our beloved Ethiopian crosses, although they are now tarnished and brown, because we believe they played a part in our survival. Looking at them takes us back to the conversation we had with the Ethiopian priest who asked us what our purpose in life was. We still don't know the answer, but we are sure it will be revealed one day. We have been so incredibly lucky to survive that we owe it to those who didn't to make the rest of our lives worthwhile.

The horrors of that tragic day will never be erased from our minds, or fully understood, but we have experienced so much generosity and hospitality that it has only confirmed our belief that most people are good and kind. Of course, there will always be bad people and there will always be politically motivated people, but it is rare to meet them as horrifically as we did. It's taken us a long time to trust strangers again. Faceless terrorists with no apparent motive have had a huge effect on our lives. The aftermath of the crash – the crowds of onlookers, media attention, conspiracy theories and the facts and fictions surrounding the event – has made us initially insecure when meeting new people. Even now we feel slightly on edge until we are confident and familiar with our situation and surroundings.

It was the worst day of our lives and nothing could ever change that, but we are now prepared to accept it. It was like a wake-up call to the important things in life which we were so keen to learn about when we initially left England. As long as we can hold on to the positive side of the experience, it can only make us stronger, kinder and more understanding of just how vulnerable we all are. We were lucky enough to be given another chance and we're not prepared to waste a second of it.

Investigating the death and destruction caused by the world's bloodiest hijack will take time. Our lawyers are still trying to ascertain what happened, and why, on that fateful day. A lot of governments are involved as there were 34 nationalities on the plane and it is further complicated by the Ethiopian government's reluctance to share any of the knowledge that they must now have.

The official line is that the hijackers were drunk, had fake passports and bought legitimate tickets. They had no bomb, apparently – only the airline axe, the fire extinguisher and the bottle of whisky. As far as we know, the

Ethiopian government has not let anyone near the black box which would, perhaps, suggest that they don't want anyone to hear what is on it.

In the absence of any more official information, we can only suggest a variety of possible scenarios. Maybe they were just drunk and wanted to go to Australia. Perhaps their motives were to do with freeing the vice-president who had recently gone down for corruption. Or they may have wanted a ransom; been involved with a recent arms deal in Ethiopia; been making a political statement because of the number of diplomats on board; were demanding the release of political prisoners; or, finally, they may have wanted political asylum themselves.

We are often asked, how many people survived. The word 'survived' seems inappropriate when some are left with broken backs or destroyed lives. Forty-seven people are still breathing and trying to put right the damage. It's not much to ask that anybody related to the dead should be able to visit their graves knowing why they died. Mass murder was committed that day and somebody should be taking responsibility.